An Extensive Life
A Life of Blessing

By
James J. Stewart

1.
My Families

On a hot summer day not long ago, while visiting a few of my descendants, I was having a conversation with one of my favorites. Her name is Samantha. She said, "Grand-dad, you should put your stories into a book. They all seem to be family history, but I'm confused as to how you know it, and where you fit in. You tell the stories as though you were there for all your stories, but that's impossible."

I wasn't sure how to respond to her because I've always told Samantha the truth. She is both brilliant and intuitive, so I answered her carefully. "Samantha, I'll tell you what. I'll write out the stories in a digitally encrypted file. The encryption key will be your birthday, with today's date, made up of six digits each, with your middle name between the two dates. Okay?"

She smiled. "Okay."

I continued with a different tone to my voice. "I'll leave the file where you can find it after my funeral."

She scowled. "Your funeral?"

"Yes, my love, I'll only be around for another year or two. Then I'm going home."

"But Grand-dad, you're not sick, and you're not old."

"That's true, Samantha, but it is getting close to my time to go home."

I changed the subject then. As I said in the beginning, that particular conversation was just this last summer. Although this is the twenty-first century, my story begins so very long ago that probably you'll find my story impossible to believe. I will translate all the early conversations into modern English for you, so my story is easier to understand. I won't tell you how to pronounce all the Scottish, Welsh, and Irish names. That's what the Internet is for.

+ + +

My mother was born in Belfast, Ireland. We were still in Belfast, on my tenth birthday, she told me that she thought she was about nineteen when I was born, but she wasn't sure.

Mother started working when she was thirteen because everyone in the family worked as soon as they were able. She worked at mopping floors in a pub near the water's edge. By the time she was fifteen, my mother was serving drinks and getting good tips because she was very good looking. She was slender, petite, and very pretty.

Late one night, there was a pounding at the door. My mother yelled, "We are closed! Go home and get some sleep!"

Through the door, she heard, "We're on our way home back to Scotland, and we just need a few beds for the night!"

It was a cold and rainy night, and my mother could not stand the idea of people being stuck out in the cold and dampness. When she unlocked the door, a baker's dozen people came in. She looked over the instant crowd. "I do not have enough beds for all of you. Some of you will have to sleep on the floor here in the pub."

As a rather tall and handsome man approached her, my mother's mouth dropped open. His voice was deep and melodious. "I am sorry, Miss. I know this is an imposition for you. By any chance, do you recognize me?"

She was suddenly and completely aware of who he was. She curtsied and bowed her head. She said, "Yes, your majesty." It was King James VI of Scotland!

Yes, yes, I know. You're thinking as you read this that it's impossible that my mother was born in the sixteenth century. Don't confuse yourself! Just let me tell my story. If you think this is impossible, my life will seem to get even more incredible as we go along, so if you don't want to believe me, that's your choice. You can either go on reading this, or you can quit. It's up to you.

My mother had helped put up stranded travelers previously, so it was not a new experience. She first took the King to a bed upstairs where she normally slept. Then she went downstairs and gave blankets to everyone else. Once that was done, she put some ale in a mug, put it on a tray with some scones, and took it upstairs to the King.

"Your Majesty, is there anything else your highness needs before retiring?"

"Thank you for the ale, my dear. How old are you?"

"My mum says I am almost twenty, Your Highness."

"You are a truly beautiful young woman. How long have you worked here?"

"You are very kind, Your Majesty. I have been working nearly seven years, sir. As a child, I simply mopped floors and did whatever I was told to do. I recognize you because I once saw you in a parade with our own Irish king. I am very pleased to meet you, Your Majesty."

"You speak very well, young lady. Have you had schooling?"

She nodded. "My father asked our priest to teach me to read, and at first I could only read Latin. Later, our priest introduced me to some items printed in English and Gaelic."

The King and my Mom conversed for a time by the light of an oil lamp. They talked about books they had read, and they drank tea. They had much in common. The next morning, King James VI of Scotland set sail to return into his country.

I was born about nine months later. If you know your history, then you know the implications of my being born in Belfast late in 1588. The Irish name my mother gave me was Brianan. My mother did not tell me at first who my father was. As her father did, she asked a priest to teach me to read. His name was Charles, and Father Charles and I became friends. We, read the Great Bible together, and he taught history and many other things to me. He also taught me what it means to be a man and, more importantly, what it means to be a gentleman.

My mother and I moved to Scotland just after my eleventh birthday, only before the new century began. We established our home above a pub she purchased in Linlithgow, a small town on the Firth of northeast Scotland, not far from Edinburgh. The waterfront always had a cool breeze, and town-folks were friendly. We loved it there. Mother served fish stew and ale in her pub, and I worked as a fisherman. Almost three years later, when I was a teenager, my father became James I in a union of Scottish and English crowns. My mother talked about writing to the King, to tell my father of me, but she never did write to him. For more than twenty years after that, my father ruled England, Scotland, and Ireland.

In 1617, my mother and I were in the crowd when my father traveled to Edinburgh, only a few dozen miles from the pub. We went to see the parade that was created in his honor.

My mother called out his given name and waved. He looked at her, but he did not seem to recognize her. Several years later, I would learn that he actually did recognize her, and he decided to provide for the boy standing next to her.

A few years passed. Two years before my mother died, I became a young fool in love, and I married a stunning Gaelic girl named Dearbhail. At first, it was a marriage of convenience, like so many marriages at the time. I wanted to have a wife and family, and she needed a husband and to get away from her parents. We worked hard to build the love that grew between us.

My mother died shortly after she saw her first grandchild. Dearbhail immediately got pregnant again. Oh, how Dearbhail loved being a mother and nursing her babies! She gave me seven boys and four daughters. She was a decent wife, and I did my best to be an excellent husband. Both she and our fifth daughter died in childbirth when my beloved Dearbhail was not yet forty.

By that time, I was a few years older of course, and by then I was also a bit wiser. After the burial services, I felt lost without my Dearbhail, but with church helping both me and my children, we continued on. There were always fish to be caught, and the market for them never seemed to fail.

Even as I write this, I find it a bit peculiar that I remember so few of my conversations with Dearbhail. She was never particularly talkative, so you would think that I would remember more of what she did actually say, but I don't. When she did talk, she spoke quietly. To the day of her death, our children were often in awe of her. She was a woman at peace with herself and with the world, under all the circumstances that I can remember.

During the months immediately following her death, it seemed like my life was a blur. I got up before dawn, got the children dressed, and then headed for the docks. I worked mindlessly hard, immersing myself in my fishing labors even more than I had before Dearbhail died. When I got home, I presided over preparing and eating our evening meal. Then I read to them from the Bible for a time before sending them off to bed. I always prayed with them before extinguishing the lamps. Sometimes I recited a poetic prayer I had written.

> My sons and my daughters, my children and more,
> Close now your eyes and have rest as before.
> Jesus, our savior with promises stored,
> Promises peace to you, joy, and still more.
> Day will come soon enough. Night has no fears,
> Reading and school work are done now my dears.
> Jesus is near you so find in Him cheer –
> Sleep now, and soon you'll find blessings appear.

Oh, how I loved my children from Dearbhail! However, time plunged on, and they grew up and moved away. All of them ended up living within a day's journey of our town's Linlithgow Castle, which was one of the Tudor estates. I seldom thought about my family name and heritage then, any more than I did in the years following.

Finally, my youngest daughter, Borgach, got married and left with her husband for Livingston, about ten miles south of me. Once again, I felt terribly lost. My home was empty, and I felt lonely without any children around. I wrote to my oldest son, Ailean, who by that time was living in Inverness, about a hundred miles north of my home in Linlithgow. In my letter, I asked him to return home, to help close up the house where he had been born.

Six weeks later, Ailean arrived and went inside to wait for me. Returning from the docks, I knew that he had arrived because of his horse tied out front. Going inside and seeing him, I was truly happy. "Ailean, my son! It is good to see you again."

"It is good to see you as well, Father. I got here as quickly as I could. I was surprised to hear you say you wanted to sell off the house."

Ailean had laid a fire, and we sat down in front of it. Taking a pot out of the fire, he poured hot water into cups, added whiskey, and squeezed in lemon juice. I stared at the fire. "Ailean, I wrote to you for two reasons." I sipped some of the Scottish hot toddy. "First, after we sell everything, I want you to share the proceeds evenly with your brothers and sisters."

"What about you, Father, do you not want to keep any of it?"

I shook my head. "No, son, I do not need it. I am moving to Cardigan, down in Wales, where I have inherited a house."

"For truth, Father?"

"For truth," I said. "I am telling you this because I want you to share a story – at least part of a story – with your brothers and sisters."

"Are you setting up business in Cardigan, Father?"

I nodded. "I will get to that, son." I took another sip of the toddy because it relaxed me, and I wanted to be totally honest with Ailean. "About a month ago, there was a fire down on the Firth. I stood in the crowd, watching it, for a long time.

"The crowd was rowdy, typical of dock workers. One of them snarled to another. 'I hope the artless milk-livered pignut that started this fire is burning inside!'

"Someone yelled a response. 'Aye! The fobbing rump-fed lout should burn in hell!'

"The fire did not spread to other buildings, but it seemed to burn endlessly. It did neither grow nor subside. All efforts to put it out failed. Suddenly, I heard a scream from inside the building. For some reason, I thought it sounded like your mother in heaven, and foolishly without thinking about it, I ran into the building and its flames."

"Who was it?"

"Just listen, my son." I took another sip of toddy. "Inside, it was not as hot as I expected. What I am about to tell you, you will find impossible to believe. I saw what appeared to be a woman in the midst of the flames. Maybe she was an angel, but I don't know for sure.

"She said, 'Brianan, our God in heaven is giving you two special gifts, and you will not know why until you go home to heaven. You will live an exceedingly long time, so long as you are faithful to The Creator. You must do your best to follow Jesus. You will be used for his name's sake and for his glory. He will use you in many places for many reasons, and you must not question the Creator's motives.'

"I nodded and said, 'I trust God.'

"Then she said, 'As soon as you can, you must sell all you have and move southwest nearly three hundred miles into Wales, to a town named Cardigan. Your earthly father has left you a home there, and you must claim it. The deed is in your name. Business will unfold for you there. Have faith, and continue to trust God. ... Now, run out, and I will let this building collapse into embers.' She disappeared. I ran out of the flames, and the building crashed down behind me."

Ailean stared at his father. "What happened then?"

"People asked me why I ran in. Feeling a bit wiser, I simply told them that I thought I heard someone scream, but that there was no one there. Son, I do not know how long I will be in Cardigan. I want you to tell your brothers and sisters that I have moved there, but do not tell any of them about the vision. When your first child turns twenty, I want you to tell that child the whole story. If he or she does not live that long, pass on the story to the next oldest. I want this to be a tradition in our family. Will you promise me to do your part?"

Ailean nodded. "I will, Father."

We sat there by the fire well into the night. We talked as only a father and son can talk. "Your mother was quiet but wise, wasn't she?"

He nodded. "Aye, Father, she was. I was in awe of her almost all the time."

"Will you continue to pray as I have taught you, kneeling and humble before our Creator?"

He nodded. "That I will, Father."

We ate. We drank, and then we drank some more. We went to our beds satiated, but we were not drunk.

It took us but a few days to sell everything. I tearfully said good-bye to Ailean one morning, after he promised to take care of a few final sales and divide all the proceeds with his siblings. We hugged and cried, and then I mounted my horse.

When I got to Cardigan on a Monday, the Town Crier took me to the large estate where there was a substantial home with my name in the deed. Inside the house, he showed me that deed.

It said that I had inherited it from my father, James Tudor. The Crier looked at me. "Are you a son of the King?"

I raised my brows. "I've never met him."

The home was a great deal larger and nicer than the one that I had sold in Linlithgow. Arrangements were in place so that a neighbor north of my property was the caretaker. His pay was the proceeds from crops grown in a field on the north side of my land. The house had some nice furnishings, including a mirror in the largest of six bedrooms.

As the Crier left in order to do his other duties, he handed me a written message from Cardigan's banker. It said that in a savings account, there was continuing to accrue a modest amount of interest. I said a silent prayer of thanksgiving. I knew that my father had recognized my mother and me in the crowd after all.

That evening, sipping some tea, I thought about my new home and how I had come to have it. Henry Frederick, the Prince of Wales, was undoubtedly my half-brother. Why he was not living in what was now my home? I did not know. The Tudor family had many properties, of course. My half-sister, Elizabeth of Bohemia, did not like Wales, or so I heard, so I did not expect to ever see her – or Henry, for that matter. My half-brother, Charles, would later become King, when my father died. I would never meet him either. That night, tired from my journey, I slept very well.

The next day, I looked into a mirror, and I was shocked. My skin was weathered and somewhat dirty, but there were no wrinkles. My hair was black as can be, with no trace of the gray that I'd had up north. That was particularly interesting because in Scotland, I had picked grey hairs out of my brush. I appeared to be younger than I had been when I left.

In another large room, I found many books of law on several shelves. At a beautiful desk, I found unopened mail. Deciding that was a good place to begin, I began opening the letters. Reading them, I saw that my business was to be that of a solicitor. In what was then called the New World, a solicitor was called a lawyer, although, as a solicitor in Wales, I had the power of a small-town judge. I began reading the law books as fast as I could, reading from dawn to dusk each day until the following Sunday.

+++

While I settled into my new home in Cardigan, my son Ailean in Linlithgow distributed the family's assets among his siblings. I can say this because he told me he would, and he was a man of his word. I received one letter from Ailean, about a year after I got established in Cardigan. Because Linlithgow Castle was one of the favorite residences of the Tudors and Stewarts, Ailean and his siblings stayed in that part of Scotland. Ailean lived the furthest north in Inverness, but he kept track of all his siblings.

Decades later, shortly before I left Wales, I was having a pint with friends when I learned about a prayer warrior in Linlithgow, or so the man was described. The description sounded like my Ailean, although the way the stories were told, I was sure it was mixed at least somewhat with gossip. According to the story, the man and his wife ran a pub in Linlithgow, and it was said that sometimes miracles happened when he led a gathering in prayer.

Before Ailean came of age and got married, he was always attentive to my prayers and asked me about things I said to God during family worship. Perhaps the stories I heard about him were true, but I will never know. There are so few records of pub life during that era of Scotland. Linlithgow is no longer such a small town, but is now much larger, almost a suburb of Edinburgh. I worked hard there, and my memories are mostly pleasant.

2.
Cardigan Arrival

That first Sunday in Cardigan was the second of many life-changing experiences. (The first was the angel in the fire in Linlinthgow.) The little church in Cardigan was quaint, with a few stained-glass windows paid for by wealthier members. The church's roof was steep and tall, and a large bell was enclosed in a cupola on the top of the front wall.

As I arrived, everyone was staring at me and whispering. I assumed that it was because I was a new resident, and no one knew me. I proceeded to introduce myself to the men as I encountered them, and they in turn introduced me to others standing nearby. I quickly learned that Cardigan's Crier had spread the word that I was a Tudor, and that had generated a wildfire of gossip.

A deacon escorted me to a pew near the front, and a few moments later the worship began. It was a beautiful service. The Vicar offered a surprisingly brilliant sermon, and I was impressed. As I was listening, I saw behind the Vicar a seemingly familiar face in the chorus, a woman who looked strikingly like the one I had seen in the flames a month or so earlier. I blinked and looked again, and I did not see her.

At the conclusion of worship, I started to make my way up the aisle, and I found myself surrounded by young women. One rather tall woman with cascades of brown hair touched my arm. "Mr. Tudor, my name is Dolidh. Are you closely related to the King?"

I shook my head. "Perhaps someday I will be able to answer that question." I continued to make my way slowly up the aisle.

A slightly younger woman put her arm through mine. She was rather petite, with blue eyes, flaming red hair, and a figure that reminded me of that of my beloved Dearbhail, by then at peace in heaven. "Mr. Tudor, does Jesus dwell within your heart, as your Savior, best friend, and constant companion?"

I looked into her eyes. It was a startlingly unexpected question, and I nodded. "Yes, He certainly dwells within my heart. Without Him there, I do not think I could now live with the void that is in my life. What about you, young lady?"

She smiled, and I felt warmer, as my heart began to beat faster. "Yes, he absolutely does, sir. He guides me and empowers me in amazing ways." She smiled once more. "Will we be seeing you in church again next week? We get so few visitors in our little town, and it is refreshing to have someone new in our parish."

I nodded. "Yes. Perhaps you and I may converse again next week."

"That would be most excellent!" She smiled again, curtseyed, and walked away.

I truly hoped to have future conversations with that strikingly attractive girl. A man approached me. "Mr. Tudor, my name is Donaidh Morgan. I wrote a letter to you when I heard you were coming to Cardigan and moving into the old Tudor estate."

I nodded. "Yes, Mr. Morgan, I read your letter this last Tuesday. As I understand it, there is a dispute over the sale of a stallion some five weeks ago."

"Yes. The man claims that the animal does not do the duties of a stallion."

I nodded. "I have an office in my home. Would coming to see me on Wednesday be a time to visit me?"

He smiled. "Indeed."

"I shall look forward to seeing you that day, mid-morning, sir."

Mr. Morgan and I chatted for a few more minutes. I hoped by then I could read up on relevant laws that can apply in his case. I continued walking towards the rear of the church.

After Donaidh Morgan said farewell to the Vicar, I shook the priest's hand and introduced myself. "Good morning! As you probably know, I am Brianan Tudor."

"Good morning! I saw you sitting there in front. You have a fine singing voice, Mr. Tudor. I am Vicar Art Moss."

Thank you, Vicar Moss. I am a new solicitor in Cardigan. I love hearing sermons from John's gospel. This morning, you certainly did the fifteenth chapter justice, Vicar."

"Thank you, you are very kind. Call me Art. Will I see you next Sunday?"

"Of course, I endeavor to worship every Sunday."

"I was amused to see the young women gathering around you. The taller young woman is Dolidh Price. As you found out, she is quite aggressively looking for a husband. She was about to be married, but her fiancé was killed last year – no, two years ago – in a winter storm just after Christmas."

I nodded. "The other one seemed to be quite peaceful. I think I saw Jesus in her face."

The Vicar smiled. "Yes, that was Sileas Rees. Except for my wife, Una, Sileas is probably the most Christ-centered woman in all of Cardigan. She is a young woman worthy your acquaintance. She got highest marks in her schooling."

I smiled. "Thank you, Art. I will see you next week. If the church does not already have a solicitor, I will work for it *pro bono.*"

"Thank you, you are very kind, Mr. Tudor."

"If I am to call you Art, you must call me Brianan. Good bye, sir." I turned and started down the steps.

"Good-bye and God bless you."

My home was less than a mile away, so at the end of the cobblestone walkway I turned left and briskly walked down the road. The air was cool, but not particularly damp that day. As my lungs filled from the exercise, I had lots of energy.

A buggy pulled up beside me and stopped. "Mr. Tudor!"

I stopped and looked at an older couple. I smiled. "Hello!"

"Hello! We met you in the chapel earlier this morning, just before the usher seated you." The man smiled. I am Ailean Thomas, and this is my wife Caitir. Would you be interested in joining us for dinner, sir? Our cook prepares plenty of food. We would like to get to know you."

I nodded. "Very well, sir, thank you."

"Step in sir, the rear seat is quite comfortable."

I did, and it turned out that their home was only about a half mile beyond my estate As we entered their home, as a butler took my hat, cape, and cane, I looked around. "This looks like a fine old estate. Has it always been in your family?"

Ailean nodded. "Oh, yes, the Thomas family has lived here for many generations. Do you find your Tudor home to your liking?"

We walked into a large living area and made ourselves comfortable. I nodded in response to his question. "It is quite comfortable. Evidently, it was a summer cottage for one of my forebeares. I just learned about my inheritance of it recently. You said your given name is Ailean. That is the name of one of my children from an early marriage. My wife died in childbirth."

He frowned. I am sorry to hear that. You must have married when you were very young."

I nodded. "Yes." I paused. "Our vicar is quite brilliant is he not? Cardigan is blessed to have such a capable man."

Caitir nodded and smiled. "Oh, yes, we are truly blessed. If I did not have my beloved, and he was not married, well, I ...." She blushed.

Ailean patted her hand and smiled. "My wife and I have been married thirty-four years. I sit on the board of the railroad, and I own a mine about eleven miles north of here."

"I see. I used to live near Edinburgh, and after my wife's death, I decided to make a fresh start. It was quite convenient to be able to set up a solicitor's practice here."

I enjoyed getting to know them, and it was late in the evening when I finally returned home. Monday was filled with studying for my first case with Donaidh Morgan, and his dispute over the sale of a stallion.

On Tuesday, I was just finishing some tea after breakfast, when, in the distance, I heard a scream. Through my window, I could see a carriage with a runaway team of horses racing along the road. I was already fully dressed, so I ran down my walkway and, as the horses ran past me, I dove for the reins dragging on the ground.

"Whoa!" I called to the horses. By the time I brought them to a halt, I had some scrapes and bruises, torn pants, and dirt all over me. I turned and looked up into the carriage. It was Sileas Rees!

"Th-thank you, Mr. Tudor! How can I ever thank you enough?! I w-was scared to death!"

I think I was smiling as I nodded. "You are welcome. I understand from the Vicar that your name is Sileas Rees."

She blushed. "Yes! I did not properly introduce myself Sunday morning." She paused. "I guess ...."

"That is quite all right. You seem to be shaking. May I drive you home?"

She nodded. "Yes, yes, thank you."

I tied her reigns just below the horsewhip. "I will get my horse and return in a few moments." I went into my barn. I saddled my horse, and coming out, I secured my horse's reigns to the back of the carriage.

Before joining her, I took a handkerchief and wiped the dust and dirt off of my face. As I climbed into the buggy, Sileas moved over and demurely leaned against the corner. I looked over at her and smiled. "I will take us slowly to your home. Where is it?"

Sileas looked extremely shy at that moment and spoke softly. "We live – rather, my family lives – on the east side of the road, straightaway, just over a mile beyond the church. Thank you. It is kind of you to do this."

"It is my pleasure." I softly whistled and laid the whip gently across the horses. They took off at a slow trot. "If you do not mind my asking, what happened?"

We rode silently a few moments before she answered. "After church on Sunday, do you remember being approached by Dolidh Price, a rather tall woman about three years older than I am?"

I nodded. "She was the first young woman to speak to me at the conclusion of worship, and you were the second."

Sileas nodded. "She is an old friend. After breakfast this morning she said she wanted to go riding. I drove this carriage while she rode alongside me on her horse. About three miles northeast of town, we began arguing about … about people in church on Sunday. Dolidh is somewhat mercurial, some might say. She became angry with me, called me a saucy tickle-brained flirt-gill, turned her horse about, and took off towards home rather rapidly."

I smiled. "It sounds like Dolidh can speak rather colorfully!"

Sileas nodded. "She can, when she's angry, but we've been friends since we were children, and I don't pay much attention."

She and I were passing the church just then, and she stopped speaking as we watched some children playing on the grass. Then she looked straight ahead again. "By the time I got this carriage turned around, she had been out of sight for a few minutes, so I put these horses into a fast trot. I went over a rut and lost control not far from your home." Sileas pointed. "That is our family's home, the white one on that hill."

I nodded. "It is quite picturesque. You must have a good staff to maintain the grounds."

"Yes, we have a loyal staff. Our family has an unusual tradition. When we need someone, we buy a slave with the appropriate qualifications and skills. Then we treat them like an extended family. After three years, we give them their freedom, and we tell them they can either stay with us or move on. Most of them have stayed and are very loyal to us. Our neighbors do not approve of our doing this, but as my father told the Vicar one day, it is the humane thing to do."

I hardly needed to signal the horses to turn up the drive. They knew their way home, and we rode silently until we reached her family's mansion entrance. A man was there to help Sileas get out of the carriage, and she smiled at him. Thank you, Alan. My team got away from me for a time, but God provided Mr. Tudor to get the carriage back under control. Please put the carriage in its place and take care of the horses."

"Yes, Miss Sileas, I will take care of it."

Once again, she put her arm through mine. "Please come inside with me. I want you to meet my parents, so we can all thank you properly." When we reached the top of the steps, her parents were there. "Father, mother, I am sure you remember seeing Mr. Brianan Tudor at church. I had a frightening experience when I lost the reigns of the carriage, but as I was passing his home, he ran after us, grabbed the reigns, and brought the carriage to a halt."

Sileas' mother stepped forward and wrapped her arms around her daughter. Her father beamed. "Praise God you are both alright! We did not introduce ourselves Sunday. Call me Andreas." We shook hands. "This is my wife, Rebecca."

She bowed, and I kissed her hand. "I am honored to meet you both."

Andreas smiled. "The honor is ours. Come with me sir. I will get you a robe to wear while we have someone repair and clean your clothing."

Rebecca touched my arm. "Please stay and join us for our mid-day meal, sir. We have had a boar roasting for several hours, and it should be quite flavorful. We also have good French wines."

I nodded my head. "Again, I will be honored." I glanced at Sileas, and she smiled.

We sat down at a large table, and I looked around at the family. It was not as large as my family had been in Linlinthgow. In our conversations, I learned that Sileas had two older brothers, an older sister, and a younger brother. Furthermore, living there were her grandparents on both her parents' sides, sitting across from me. With everyone at the table, Andreas said a prayer, and the rather noisy meal began. As they were being served, Andreas looked at their guest. "Brianan, I understand you are a solicitor."

"Yes, sir, I am. I already have some customers. One of them is *pro bono*, of course, because it is our church."

Rebecca raised her glass. "What does *pro bono* mean?"

I raised my glass to her. "It is a Latin phrase meaning 'for the public good.' In this case, I will not charge the church any fees for my services, if and when needed." I glanced at Sileas, and she subtly blushed.

Alan nodded. "By contrast, I would expect you to charge appropriate fees to the town council, when necessary, because we levy taxes to pay government expenses. Cardigan has needed to have its own solicitor, so you are heaven-sent. Apart from you, Brianan, the next closest solicitor is many leagues from here."

I chewed and swallowed before responding. "It is good to know that the town of Cardigan will be one of my clients. Are you on the town council?"

Alan smiled. "Yes. I am currently the Chairman. In most people's eyes, I am simply known as the mayor."

The meal continued with lively conversation for nearly two hours. After dessert, Alan and Brianan were given snifters of Benedictine, and they went to Alan's study to relax. As they sat down, Alan settled into his chair comfortably. "After that large meal, it seems we both have ample sufficiency."

I smiled and nodded. "This is the first time I have had a multiple course meal like that for about three years." I raised the snifter. "This is also the first time I have had Benedictine since my mother worked in a pub when I was younger. My mother told me that it was distilled from a wine made with more than twenty spices. It is excellent."

"Thank you. Since you are a Tudor, I am sure you must know your lineage, do you not?"

I hesitated, not wanting to reveal too much of myself. "Before I can answer that question properly, I have a mystery on my hands. I do not wish to appear foolish. According to Cardigan's Crier, my home is one of the several cottages among the Tudor estates. My mother told me a little about my father, as well as about my grandparents, but unfortunately some of the information was conflicted. I have been working to sort it out for quite some time. I have no doubt that I am related to James I of England in some way. He is also James VI of Scotland, of course."

"What is the mystery?"

"The deed is absolutely authentic, and my home is a bequest, but from whence did my bequest come? I have some ideas, but the mystery will take some time to unravel. I am afraid I must see to the needs of my clients as my first priority. Solving the mystery may have to wait."

Alan seemed satisfied by my answer. "I am glad you were there when Sileas needed you."

I nodded. "I am as well." Tell me, sir, would you object to my courting Sileas?"

Alan chuckled. "Of course not! She told me Sunday evening that she was hoping you would do so. Move slowly, my new friend. Sileas is not fragile, but she is precious."

"Yes, sir, and thank you, sir."

+ + +

We followed the rules of seventeenth-century courtship. Each afternoon, unless it was raining, we traveled about in the Cardigan area, always chaperoned by the driver of our courting carriage. Only the driver faced forward and controlled the horses. We faced to the rear. Since I was a Tudor, and Sileas was the daughter of a rich mayor, we had to behave properly. We talked quietly as we rode together each day, and gradually our conversations became more relaxed and increasingly intimate.

My solicitor business began to thrive, and as a follower of Jesus, I took care to give ten percent of my proceeds to the Vicar. My account at the bank began to grow dramatically.

Our courtship was quite formal and public, following Welsh traditions and devoid of almost all physical contact. Sileas and

I finally had our first kiss when the Vicar told me it was time to kiss the bride. Later, I was told that while we kissed there was loud cheering, but neither of us noticed it. It was a beautiful day in early September, the fourth to be exact. When the ceremony was over, there were food and drink at the front of the chapel, and there were a quartet and dancing in the street.

One more wedding tradition remained. The ladies in the wedding party took the bride to my home, which had been thoroughly cleaned and prepared by my groomsmen. The ladies helped Sileas get out of her dress, bathed her, and put her in my bed. While that was happening, I gave some cash to the Vicar and the musicians, and we had a final toast. The groomsmen walked with me to my home. As the groomsmen and I entered, the ladies of the wedding party came out of my bedroom and joined the rest of the party, while I went in and got into bed with Sileas. I had to do so quickly, because in less than five minutes, the entire wedding party joined us in the bedroom. Everyone wished us well. The Vicar pronounced another blessing, and everyone but Sileas and I left.

We kissed for the second time and held each other, as we listened to the giggles and laughter fading into the evening. There was pink light from the sunset, which was fading on the sheer curtains. At last, there was silence, with flickering light from a candelabra hanging above us. I looked into Sileas' eyes. "At last! Are you tired?"

"Not too tired to have some fun starting a family!" That first night I learned that she could be rather energetic and enthusiastic, and less quieter than usual. We had lots of fun.

Dawn's early light was breaking against the window when we got up and took a bath together. After some tea and scones, Sileas and I returned to bed and slept soundly.

3.
Solicitor Servant

We slept until early afternoon the day after our wedding. Then Sileas fixed us a hearty meal. I was reminded again that she was an excellent cook. I went into my study to prepare some paperwork for Mr. Morgan because he had an appointment with me for the following morning.

Later, as the sun was getting low in the sky, I returned to our living area to find that Sileas had prepared tea and scones. As we sat in front of the fire, I looked into her beautiful eyes. "I have a story to tell you, my love, but you must promise me never to repeat it to anyone."

"I cannot even share it with my father or mother?"

"No, my beloved Sileas, you must promise me absolute secrecy."

She gazed at me intently. "Very well, Brianan, I promise."

"Excellent. As I told you, before coming to Cardigan, I lived in a small town on the northeast coast of Scotland."

"It is called Linlithgow, is it not?"

"Yes. One day, about a year ago, I was working on the docks there, when a fire erupted in a large building nearby. A bucket brigade was begun, but it was of little use. Strangely, though the flames burned intensely, the building was not being consumed as one would expect. I heard a scream, and I thought it sounded like the woman who had been my wife before she died. Without thinking twice, I foolishly ran into the building." Sileas nodded silently. "Inside, it was very warm but not hot, and I did not see anyone at first. What happened next seems impossible even now, as I tell you about it."

"What happened?"

"I saw what I think was an angel. She – I do not think it was a male – was in the midst of the flames but not consumed by them. The angel spoke to me."

"Brianan, our God in heaven is giving you a special gift. You will live an exceedingly long time, so long as you are faithful to The Creator,

but you must do your best to follow Jesus. You
will be used for his name's sake and for his
glory. He will use you in many places for many
reasons, and you must not question the
Creator's motives. As soon as you can, you
must sell all you have and move to Wales, to a
town named Cardigan. Your father has left a
home there for you, and you must claim it. The
deed is in your name. Business will unfold for
you there. Have faith, and trust. Now, run out,
and I will let this building collapse into
embers."

I took a swallow of my tea. "She totally disappeared. I rapidly
ran out of the flames, and the building came down behind me."

"That is nothing short of incredible, Brianan."

I nodded. "Yes, my love. Do you understand why you must
not repeat my story to anyone?"

"Yes."

"I have told the story to only one other person – my oldest
son from my first marriage in Linlinthgow. He has promised me
to tell it only to his oldest when the time is right."

"Will I ever meet him?"

"I do not know. It seems unlikely, but since we were quite
close after his mother died, he may travel here someday to
visit."

"What was her name?"

I stared at the fire a moment, and then I answered softly.
"She was a stunningly beautiful Gaelic girl named Dearbhail. I
never thought I would meet a more beautiful girl than Dearbhail
until my first Sunday here in Cardigan, when I met you."

Sileas snuggled closer to me. "Is this your way of telling me
that you think I am beautiful?"

I laughed. "You are impossibly, wonderfully, incredibly
beautiful. I think I fell in love with you the first time you put your
arm in mine in church."

She was quiet for several moments. "The angel said that
your business will unfold here. Do you think we are going to
prosper?"

"I certainly hope so! God has set me up as a solicitor, and
I will do my best. I have to trust God with the rest. This brings us
to something else we should talk about. I want us to set aside

time every day for reading scriptures and praying together. There is a copy of the Geneva Bible in my study."

Sileas nodded. "The Vicar has called upon me to read scriptures on Sunday morning a few times. I have felt very honored."

"Your mentioning the Vicar reminds me of something. I am expecting a letter from London, perhaps as early as this week." I paused as Sileas put more tea in my cup. "I wrote to the Archbishop of Canterbury over a month ago. I appealed to him to raise the office of Vicar Art Moss. He is so much more than a Vicar here, and he deserves a higher title. More than three pages of my letter were used to describe my multiple reasons to appeal on behalf of the Vicar. Your father, as Chairman of Cardigan's Town Council, attached his own note to my letter. I am sure that the answer to my letter has been delayed because of the widespread turmoil generated by Our King's edicts."

"I overheard my parents talking about how unpopular King Charles is becoming. He is not at all like his father, James."

"We may be headed for civil war. I hope not. If fighting breaks out into the open, many innocent people will be hurt. I hope we get our answer from the Archbishop before things get too bad."

Sileas smiled. "If the letter comes when you are not here, I will put it in a safe place. Meanwhile, since we do not yet have children under our feet, it would seem best to pray and read scriptures together each evening before bed."

I nodded.

+ + +

During the next six months, Sileas and I became even more devoted to each other. Looking back, I think much of that devotion arose out of our praying for one another as well as with each other. We also spent increasing amounts of time reading our Geneva Bible and discussing what we read. I was often amazed at Sileas' brilliant understanding and interpretation of God's word.

As with most small towns, Cardigan was plagued with gossip. One evening, we were reading the book of Proverbs, and we came across this verse [Proverbs 26:20]:

Without wood, the fire is quenched, and without a talebearer strife ceaseth.

Sileas put her hand on mine. "I would like to frame this and put it on one of our walls."

I smiled. "I have noticed at church how you are attentive to what others are saying, but you do not participate in the gossip conversations."

She nodded. "I can get some parchment paper from the store and letter this verse for display. If I do so, will you be so good as to frame it?"

I kissed her on the cheek. "I would be happy to, my dear."

"I think I might be with child." She paused when I grinned. "We are both very involved in Cardigan affairs. We are going to need help."

I nodded. "I agree. Tomorrow I will hire some workers to begin enlarging our home. Do you think two more bedrooms for our children and two for servants will be sufficient?"

"It might just be a first step." She smiled. "We have enough bedrooms for now, but the children will need a place to play inside the house. May we purchase some books and start a library?"

I had to chuckle. "Yours are good ideas. You will be a good mother." I paused. "I examined the details of our deed again last week. I will not say this to your father, but we have more land than he does!"

Her eyes grew wide. "Do we own part of the forest behind us?"

"We own all the forest, along with the meadow beyond and down to Cardigan Bay on the Irish Sea. It seems that our Town Crier either did not read the entire deed, or he has maintained a big secret!"

Late the next morning, Sileas packed a picnic basket, and we began walking towards the forest. With the sun warming our backs, the breeze was almost pleasant – though still chilly as it came off of the North Atlantic.

As we entered the forest, Sileas began talking quietly. "There is something I want to show you, about fifty yards west and thirty yards north of here."

"Is it an interesting tree?"

"No, something far more significant. When you went with my father to Pembroke last month, I went walking through the forest to meditate."

"You should not have gone by yourself."

"I have been walking in this forest since I was eight years old. I used to sneak out of the house to go into the forest and be with God." She paused and pointed. "We will go up this little hill, and before we get to the top we will turn right and go around and down."

About five minutes later we came to a large jumble of downed trees piled up twice my height. "I wonder what all these logs are piled up here for."

"I wondered that for a long time, until one day I made a discovery." She pointed. "That spot right there, do you see it? Do not let your shadow cover it, but stand so that sunlight shines on it. Stoop low and look."

At first, I could not see anything. Then I peered more intently into the darkness. "There is an opening under all of this debris!"

"Yes! You are the first person to whom I have ever shown this. This is my own secret, Brianan. Dolidh and I swore each other to keep this a secret. When I was much smaller, I crawled in there. It is a large cave, and there is a spring inside with fresh water. I have not been able to get in there for several years now because I am taller, and the logs have settled." She put her hand in mine. "Come, my husband, I have one more thing to show you before we have our picnic."

We went up to the top of the hill, where there was a large but dead oak tree. The wind was brisk and steady there at the top. From there we could see parts of Cardigan as well as the ocean to the west and below us. Sometimes the wind seemed unusually noisy up there. We began to get cold.

Sileas pointed at the top of the tree "As children, Dolidh Price and I used to come up here and play. We call this tree the whistling oak because of the sound it makes when the wind is blowing more from the southwest rather than the west." She pointed down at the ground. "Dolidh and I swore each other to secrecy regarding both this oak and the cave. The roots of this oak evidently go deep down, into the hill. Inside the cave, we could look up when the sun is shining outside, and we could faintly see light up through the trunk. Inside, air blows in the opening below and out through the trunk of the tree. I do not know why, but it is true."

I put my arm around her. "We are getting cold. Let us go back and eat our picnic at home, shall we?"

She nodded. "Agreed."

We headed down the hill and turned east towards our house. "Sileas, last evening you told me that there is increased talk among the ladies from the church regarding unrest and possible civil war."

"Yes. As I have listened, I have heard almost nothing positive said about King Charles. Two ladies said that their husbands thought that Charles will be forcibly removed from his throne. That would be bad, would it not?"

I nodded. "Yes. I have already heard about skirmishes. It seems we are on the verge of civil war. We should pray and ask God what we should do."

She was quiet. "That seems the right thing to do. Do you think there are some men in town we can trust with complete confidence?"

We walked for a few minutes before I answered. "I believe we can trust your father, do you agree?"

"Yes, I know we can."

"Good. We have four days before Sunday. You will be speaking with your mother before then. Does your mother gossip?"

"No! Never! She despises gossip."

"I thought so. If you and your mother happen to talk about having family dinner there after church on Sunday, you and I can perhaps sit down for some serious talk with your parents."

As we approached the house, Sileas was quiet and thoughtful. "I am pleased that you trust my parents as I do, Brianan. Are we going to talk to them about the cave?"

We stopped on the rear porch of our home, and I looked into her eyes. "Our minds are alike in this, Sileas. We have much to pray about, do we not?"

"Yes, beloved."

Inside the house, Sileas stoked and built up the fire to heat water for tea. I spread out our picnic food on the table. Then I went into my study, and I started reading our Bible. Shortly, Sileas came in and said, "Our tea is ready, Brianan. Shall we eat?"

"Yes." I followed her to the table, and we stopped to hold hands and pray. "Father, thank you for this food and for the love we share. In both the books of Joshua and Samuel, I found instances where caves were used for security in times of war.

Please guide our minds and hearts as we consider the future that you have prepared for us. In Jesus' name, we pray. Amen."

"Amen." As we sat down, she said, "You have not been inside the cave yet, so you do not know details about it yet. Several times, Dolidh and I lit torches and carried them into the cave. There is a large central chamber, and there are four smaller lower chambers."

I chewed a piece of crocked venison and sipped some tea. "Are all the chambers tall enough for adults to stand?"

She nodded. "The large main chamber has a ceiling of at least twenty feet I think. Three of the smaller chambers are six to seven feet tall. One is about four feet tall." She bit into a scone and sipped her tea. "If all the chambers were on the same level side by side, the total area would be at least three times the size of our house."

I put my cup down and goggled at her. "This is for true?"

She nodded. "Cardigan Castle is of course much larger. Everyone knows where it is, and an army can besiege it."

We continued to eat. I had not considered the possibility that the cave was that large. With civil war looming as a strong possibility, we discussed the cave as a real asset. Unlike his father, King James, Charles I was arrogant and disruptive.

As we had eaten nearly all that she had prepared, she poured more tea for us. "Thank you." I looked at her. "We have old clothes that we can work in, and we can wear additional undergarments if we go out before dawn tomorrow. We will need gloves. I will put my axe and a saw in the cart. Furthermore, some oil for torches will be needed."

"Some people may ask why we did not buy wood as usual instead of gathering it for ourselves. We can say it was an adventure we could do together. What is your plan?"

"We will eat some breakfast before we depart. We will drive the cart to the edge of the woods. Once there, we will first go into the forest and make a way into the cave before there is much of day's light. We shall not want it exposed to the knowledge of others who may wander there. We will be careful to do what we must do before others might see us. We should not take more than an hour to explore the inside. Then we will fill the cart with wood. You will gather smaller branches, and I will cut larger logs. If anyone sees us coming home, it will look like we were simply gathering wood for fuel."

She nodded. "Later, when the sun begins setting, shall we read scriptures and pray until we are sleepy?"

I nodded. "That is a good plan. Meanwhile, we both have work to do before tomorrow."

+ + +

In the months that followed, Sileas truly became my partner in serving God. As we prayed with each other and for each other, we gradually came to think alike in many things. We also learned to trust each other to know God's leading in our lives.

Once we had created a secret doorway, we began taking lamps with us when we went into the cave. The cave complex turned out to be even larger than Sileas had said. There was a total of eleven chambers. The chamber most distant from our entrance was much deeper, and it had a large opening in the cliff overlooking the beach and sea below. That opening was another reason the entire cave always had fresh air.

We took Sileas' parents and Ailean and Caitir Thomas from the church into our confidence. When Dolidh got married, Sileas insisted that she and her new husband, Arawn Stewart, join our little cave clan. That is what we began to call our secret group. Each time any of us went to the cave, we were careful not to take the same route as we had previously. The property of Andreas and Rebecca also bordered on the forest and the river, so there were several routes with variations.

We began storing emergency supplies of food in the cave, as well as storing other provisions. As it turned out, Andreas had learned some special skills from Ailean Thomas and his owning mines nearby. We furnished it to be a home way from home, yet with all the work that the eight of us were putting into it, we managed to keep our secret.

Sileas and I had been married seven months when she decided that she was definitely pregnant. It made us both blissfully happy. As women within the church began supplying us with baby clothing and diapers, the men began working with me to enlarge the house.

Once construction was completed, I went to Gloucester to hire some servants. I found a man and woman with excellent references, and when we had journeyed back to Cardigan, we found that Sileas and Rebecca had furnished the servants' quarters very well. The servants immediately liked Sileas. His name was Baodan, and hers was Bethan. He had been in the King's army about a year but had resigned his commission. She was a cook for the army, where she met him before he resigned his commission. They had been married about a year.

Bethan could not have children, but my very pregnant Sileas and Bethan quickly became friends. At that time, Andreas and Rebecca did not yet take their servants into their confidence regarding the cave. Sileas and I decided to pray about it.

Our first child was a girl, and we named her Owena. Everyone doted on her, including Dolidh, who was pregnant. The church's nursery, which had not had any babies for five years, was being used again.

By the time Sileas and I had been married a year, I no longer had thoughts of Dearbhail and the children in Scotland except at Christmas. On Christmas Eve, the church was especially full. Sileas was nursing Owena, and sitting next to her Dolidh was nursing her first child, a boy named Dylan. Vicar Art Moss had become a bishop. The Archbishop of Canterbury had responded to my plea.

As we ate our feast in the church hall, Sileas leaned toward me and spoke softly. "What were you and the bishop talking about so intensely? When others are home celebrating Christmas, will we be otherwise occupied, my husband? I wonder about what is happening outside of Cardigan, don't you?"

I also spoke softly. "There was fighting yesterday at Swansea. Things have been quiet today, and, tomorrow being Christmas, we doubt that there will be fighting."

"This is now civil war, is it not?"

I nodded. "So it appears." I looked across the room at Andreas, and when I caught his eye, I nodded and wiped my brow with my napkin. He cocked his head to the right, and tugged on his ear. He turned and whispered to Rebecca, and she nodded. During the rest of the dinner, from time to time, I could see the signal being passed.

After the dinner, Sileas, Owena, and I rode in the back of our carriage, with Baodan driving and Bethan beside him in front. We went back to our home, but rather than putting the carriage in the barn, we stopped in front. "Baodan?" I spoke quietly.

"Yes, sir?"

"Leave the carriage here for now. We will all go inside. There is something that we must discuss before retiring for the evening."

He nodded, and he and Bethan tied up the horses. Sileas and I went inside with Owena. Our fire was barely embers, but I quickly built it up so that water could be heated for tea. As our servants came in, I called out. "Baodan, Bethan, come join Sileas and I for some tea."

4.
Civil War

When we all had our cups of tea, we sat near the fire. It was a cold evening, but Bethan was smiling. "It is so nice, sir, on Christmas Eve, to be gathering with the faaround to have tea."

Baodan looked at her, and then he looked at the three of us. "Yes, we appreciate how you have made us part of your family."

Sileas smiled. "Yes, and we are glad to share Christmas with you."

I nodded. "First, I am going to offer a Christmas prayer." I paused and closed my eyes. "Heavenly Father, all praise and glory belong to you. We remember, O God, when hope and anticipation were wonderfully met by the light of one bright star that first Christmas, and the joy of discovery at that time. Our Messiah, Savior, and King was born in the humblest of places. Lord, the wise men and shepherds saw you and knew whom they had met, and they saw and fell down on their knees in adoration. Around this fire, we meet and imagine the stable and the manger. In these quiet moments of prayer this Christmas Eve, we pause once again after worship and dinner at the church to remember the smell of the hay, the sound of the animals, the cry of that precious baby you sent into the world. Draw us close to our Savior Messiah and King as we bring not gold or frankincense, but the gift of our lives the only offering we can bring. Draw us close to you, Lord, and to each other, and we discuss what lies ahead for us. We ask this in Jesus' name, Amen."

"Amen." Sileas and the others sipped their tea. She was solemn. "Brianan and the bishop talked intensely and quietly at the dinner tonight."

I nodded. "There was fighting yesterday at Swansea. Soldiers are doing some pillaging along the way. Today being Christmas Eve, things have been quiet. Tomorrow being Christmas, I doubt that there will be fighting. You know as well as we do that since Charles became King there have been problems. We've all heard about the skirmishes that have grown closer and closer to Cardigan."

Sileas spoke quietly. "Brianan and I began preparing against the possibility of civil war many months ago. As we've gotten to know you, we have also come to trust you. We know that you will not betray our trust, and that is very important."

Baodan nodded. "We are glad you trust us, and we trust you as well. It appears our mutual trust has become significant."

I nodded. "Yes. We have been building upon a secret for many months. Sileas and I have not told you about it until now, because the fewer people there are that know about it, the safer all of us are. We know that if an organized army approaches this area, Cardigan Castle will be attacked. Sileas and I decided quite some time ago that there is a safer place to be, so long as only a limited number of people know about it."

Baodan scowled. "There is a safer place than Cardigan Castle?"

"Yes. When you put the carriage in the barn tonight, release all the horses to the pasture but the old mare. Keep her in her stall, and have the cart ready to leave easily in the semi-darkness before dawn." When Baodan nodded, I continued. "Bethan, you and Baodan still have that nice large trunk. Fill it with clothing for the two of you, along with anything you do not want to take the chance of being lost to war."

She nodded. "Are we leaving tomorrow?"

I smiled. "If everything proceeds as planned, the five of us are leaving either just after sunset tomorrow or early the following morning."

Sileas stood up. "Now that we've finished our tea, there are more preparations for tomorrow. After morning worship, we will still have our Christmas dinner in the early afternoon, but at my parents' home." The rest of us stood up. "We will have to decide what we are leaving behind. Hopefully, we will be able to return to our home here and find it little damaged. We must face the possibility that we might not."

I nodded. "Baodan, we will leave enough room in the cart for your trunk, but we will fill up the remaining space with cushions and pillows early tomorrow morning. Sileas and I will transport our trunk tomorrow evening. I tell you this now, so that you and Bethan may plan for the morning."

There was little talk for the rest of the evening. Sileas was so very wise and brilliant. She and I decided not to tell them about the cave, but show them when we got there. Baodan and Bethan completed their nightly duties before beginning to pack their trunk.

+ + +

Christmas worship was always such a joyous time at the church. During those two hours, we put aside our concerns of civil war to focus on the Christmas story recorded in the Bible. We put ourselves into the music as well. I joined a men's chorus that morning to sing the Christmas music we knew so well. 1644 was drawing to a close in a week, but Bishop Art Moss focused on the day. He wove together the current dynamics of civil war with the dynamics of Mary and Joseph's story. It was brilliant.

After the worship service, everyone in the "cave clan" quietly wished one another a blessed Christmas, while acknowledging what they would do before the end of the day. Sileas, Owena, and I joined Andreas and Rebecca in their carriage, all of us looking forward to a traditional Christmas dinner. Andreas was enthusiastic and full of joy. "Bishop Moss was in fine form this morning, don't you think, son?"

I had to admit it. "It was a fine – a brilliant – homily, Andreas. He had to acknowledge the dogs of war are nearby in the midst of this joyous season."

Less than an hour later, the growing family sat down to a traditional Scottish Christmas dinner. After Andreas said a beautiful Christmas prayer of blessing, we started with carrot and coriander soup with bits of smoked salmon.

Knowing that this might be their last truly filling meal for some time, Rebecca had seen to it that there were several dishes to sample for their main course, including roast turkey, roast potatoes, roast parsnips, chestnut stuffing, bacon rolls and chipolata sausages. Vegetables included Brussel sprouts, carrots, and peas, served with gravy, bread sauce and cranberry jelly. Just when Sileas and I thought there could not be any more foods to sample, the servants brought out roast Angus beef, roast pork, roast goose, venison, salmon, chicken, and pheasant.

The previous week I had talked with the Town Crier, so I shared with them some of what I had learned. "Ethan the Crier told me a few days ago, that King Charles was ignoring the threat of civil war and making things worse. Then I asked about news from Europe and the New World. He said more colonies are being established there, south of a community called New York."

Andreas looked up from his plate. "Indeed, there are still more colonies being established?"

I nodded. "After the Puritans established some communities, there have been more being established further south along the coast of the Atlantic Ocean, and communities are developing further inland. I have sent a letter to a friend in Glasgow, who is an exporter. I've asked him for more information. I am very curious."

For dessert, we had our choice of Christmas pudding or Clootie Dumpling. Sileas chose a Clootie Dumpling, and I chose the Christmas Pudding, but then we ate off of each other's plates.

Andreas and I put on our coats and took our brandy outside to talk. He spoke quietly. "You know my servant, Alan. I would trust him with my life. That's important as the war grows close to us. Just after sundown he will go and lay a fire in the cave. He and my other servants have made their way in the dark a number of times. After dark, they will release our animals, so we can all move into the cave."

I took a sip of the brandy. "I've not made similar arrangements with Baodan and Bethan, but Sileas and I know the way. What about the others?"

"Dolidh knows the way just as well as Sileas, of course. She will see to it that everyone who should be with us will join us."

I thought for a few moments before I spoke again. "I think that to be safe, we should do no cooking during the daytime. Even if soldiers do not see our smoke, they might smell the aromas of food."

Andreas nodded. "I agree. We should also have a guard posted during the day each day, don't you think?"

I shook my head. "No. We cannot take a chance that our guard would be seen from a distance before he saw them."

Andreas nodded. "Very well, that makes sense. The women will play games with the children during the day, and we men can read to everyone at night."

+ + +

Using his mining experience, Andreas had installed curtains for all the doorways into the smaller caves. Next to the fire pit, a stove had been built, and nearby was a table with pots, pans, and utensils.

The cave that was the bedroom for Sileas, Owena, and me was small, but we had a makeshift bed with plenty of blankets, a table, and some shelves for my books. The other families had similar provisions. Months of planning and preparing became fulfilled that Christmas night.

It was very late when Sileas and I snuggled together on our pad that was to be our bed. "Brianan, how long do you think we will have to be here?"

I thought for a moment. "I actually have no idea. We could be here for as little as a week or as long as several months. Our initial supplies will keep us reasonably well fed for about three weeks. The children were all asleep when we got here. They don't know if we traveled all night or a few minutes."

She sighed. "That's good. I will pass the word that we won't tell the children how close we are to home. It is going to be a challenge to keep Owena and the other children occupied. Dolidh is a good teacher, but the children cannot have school every day."

"We will worship every morning and evening. Bishop Art has made plans. Your friend, Mary, has brought a recorder to help us with music, and I heard someone playing a lute."

We slept soundly, but I awakened to thunder in the distance. When fully awake, I realized it was not thunder. Sileas was still sound asleep, so I tried not to awaken her as I quickly dressed.

Going to the outer door, I opened it just a crack. There was barely the light of pre dawn. South of us, towards Cardigan Castle, I saw a flicker of light, and a few seconds later I heard the thunder of what was probably a canon.

I heard Ailean's voice behind me. "Is it Cardigan Castle?"

"Yes. That is canon fire, not thunder."

I closed the door and latched it. Then I turned. "We might as well just wait."

"Yes, I think you're right. Many of my employees are taking refuge in the mines. Andreas arranged for others to join them.

My workers know their way around so well in the mines. They can defend themselves there for weeks if necessary."

We went back into the main cave. The stove was already hot, and Bishop Art was making tea. "Is it Cardigan Castle?"

"Yes."

Those first cups of tea marked the beginning of our staying in the cave for nine weeks. No one went out the door into the forest. Those wanting to go outside could go to the cave chamber with the opening in the cliff. We also dumped our human waste down the cliff there.

Life in the cave was not easy. The adults focused on keeping the children occupied and entertained. When we heard distant sounds of fighting, we talked about being safe in the cave. When the sounds of war faded, we emphasized patience, and then we would hear the sounds return. During the nights, sometimes one of us would open the door cautiously, and usually, there were one or more places that glowed from fires.

Finally, when we had not heard the sounds of war for several days, there was a full moon. I sent Baodan into town that evening to spy out the area. He did not return until just before dawn. The men got into the habit of having early-morning tea together and praying with each other.

I greeted Baodan when he returned. "Good morning to you, Baodan, what did you learn?" I handed him a cup of tea.

"Good morning, and thank you, Brianan, the damage is not severe outside of the castle. Though it was cold, with the full moon, I never lit a lantern. There are a few broken windows, and the doors of some houses are standing open, but the main damage is to Cardigan Castle. Its gates did not hold."

"Are you sure?"

"Yes, I went into it, and there was no one there."

Andreas was intense. "Has the fighting left the area?"

Baodan nodded and took another swallow of tea. "I went down to the pub in the lower town. No one knows me there. I told them I was passing through and asked about the fighting. I was told that all the fighting was shifting northwards and out of our beloved Wales. One man said that there had been fighting up northward in Llangrannog, but that everything is peaceful there now."

Bishop Art spoke firmly. "I think we should proceed as planned. After the younger children are asleep this evening, we will take our several different routes to our homes. We've already talked to the older children about keeping the location of this cave a secret. This is Thursday, so we will come together again at the church on Sunday. We've agreed on our stories, so we will stick with them."

Andreas nodded. "Yes, and if fighting breaks out nearby once again, we know where we will be safe. Let us restock this cave over the next few days in case it is needed again."

We all nodded.

The families went into different directions. Some went south towards St. David, and some went east, like Andreas and Rebecca. They went as far as Brecon.

Sileas and I took Owena and our servants north an hour after the sky turned black, and the nearly full moon rose. Taking our time, we went past Tywyn before turning around. It was shortly before dawn when we stopped at a tavern in Tywyn to have some tea and a small breakfast. We explained that we were returning to Cardigan after finding shelter during the fighting. We were vague about whether our shelter was a cave or an abandoned mine.

After breakfast, we picked up the pace of our traveling and arrived in Cardigan in the mid-afternoon. As we stopped in front of our house, I was pleased to see that there was no visible damage. Sileas and Bethan went into the house, while Baodan and I took the carriage to the barn. As he and I stopped, Baodan pointed across the pasture. "It looks like we've not lost our livestock, praise God! After I take care of the mare and give her a good brushing, I will feed the others."

I nodded. "Excellent, my friend, you do that while I go into the house and see if we've lost anything."

As I went in, Sileas greeted me with a kiss. "We don't see any damage. I don't think any soldiers came in here, praise God! We've a bit of food that we left in the basement for our meal and tea. Bethan and I will give the house a good cleaning tomorrow."

I nodded. "That seems to be a good plan for the rest of the day. I will now check our postal receptacle to see if we have anything there. Then I will go into town and try to replenish our supplies. You have plenty to do here."

The remainder of the week, all of us were very busy. By Sunday morning, everything seemed to be close to normal again. At the worship service, we found that most people had returned before we did. The church was nearly full. On the previous day, the Town Crier had announced a pot luck supper after church. Following worship, we shared food and fellowship. Those of the cave clan did mostly listening. We had agreed to be vague about where we had hidden ourselves.

I was surprised to learn that I had a good deal of business awaiting me as a solicitor. Several families, in moving out of town during the fighting, had discovered that they had misplaced or lost their records of property ownership. I realized that I was going to be very occupied.

Andreas approached me as the women were cleaning up after the meal. "Brianan, do you think we'll need to bring in a magistrate for some of your cases?"

I nodded. "It seems more than simply possible. Several families had records stored in vaults in the castle. Very little seems to be left there, so I will have to help people gather witnesses to appear before a court to establish ownership."

"I took the deeds to my home with me when we left, so those things are secure for us. I'm beginning to think that Cardigan needs to establish itself as a town with borders, with its own records of ownership."

I was thoughtful. "To do what you are suggesting will undoubtedly be a long process. As a solicitor, I can declare some of what you are requesting. The court of common pleas can grant more of a legal framework. For the immediate future, that may be all that we need. Ultimately, such records need to be established with The Crown. That will be a much more permanent solution."

His face darkened. "This civil war – or a series of wars – could go on for years before The Crown issues such a decree."

"I agree. Like I said previously, it will be a long process, unless...."

"Unless?"

"Unless we can secure a friend of The Crown that will help us. With your connections, Andreas, you may know someone like that."

Andreas nodded. "I will give that some thought."

5.
Life Refreshed

An influential friend was found through an unexpected source. Dolidh Price Stewart had wanted to marry quickly, and did not know her husband Arawn very well at the time of the wedding. During their months in thewanted than a year later, they had the time to get to know one another much better, particularly their family histories. All Stewarts, as with the Tudors, were in some way related to the King. Arawn's first cousin, James, was related closely enough to live in the palace. I never told anyone that I was the bastard son of a popular previous king.

When I learned about the relationship from Sileas, we invited Dolidh and Arawn to join us for dinner after worship one Sunday. That dinner marked a new beginning for both of our families.

After I offered a blessing for our food, Baodan and Bethan began serving. I looked at Arawn as I spoke. "I am glad that you and Dolidh are able to join us today. Our wives have been friends since they were children. While taking refuge in the caves, Sileas and I felt as though we got to know the two of you better, and we want to enrich our friendships."

Sileas smiled. "Yes, I know Dolidh and my husband very well indeed, but the time at the cave gave me an opportunity to listen to you, Arawn, and to discover some of the qualities that have held the attention of your wife and my friend."

Arawn wiped his mouth on his napkin. "You are both very kind. I understand that you, Brianan, being a Tudor, are possibly more closely related to the royal family than I am, but you do not often claim that distinction. Is there a reason for that? I don't wish to offend you by prying unnecessarily." He picked up his goblet of wine and drank.

I nodded. "Since we are friends here, I will take you into my confidence. My mother was born in Belfast. At the age of thirteen, she began working in a pub there. When I was ten, she told me that when she was about eighteen, on a cold and rainy night after the pub was closed came a knock on the door. When she recognized that the person knocking was King James VI of Scotland, she let him in with his friends. She gave me few details of that night except to say that I was born nine months later."

"Really!" Dolidh's eyes were wide.

Sileas smiled. "Yes, really, and there's more, but both of you must maintain our secret with us." They both nodded.

Arawn had stopped eating, but started again. "Please continue."

I nodded. "Several years later, he was in a parade where my mother and I saw him. When she called out his given name, he turned to look at us briefly, but we did not think he recognized her. We were wrong. Some years later, after both my mother and my first wife had died, I learned about this property, and that is why I moved here and met my beautiful Sileas. I have no desire to live a privileged or royal life, so Sileas and I live here. Recently, Arawn, I learned that you have a cousin who lives in the palace."

Arawn nodded. "So long as we are being confidential and honest here as friends, I will tell you that I too am like you, Brianan, in that I have no desire to live the privileged life. My cousin, however, enjoys it."

"When we returned from the caves, Andreas asked me if it were possible to establish an area of Wales near Cardigan Bay that is a legal entity. Whatever we would call the entity, we would keep records of people and property for legal protections. In essence, I told him that without support from the Crown or a friend of the Crown, that it would take a very long time for that to come about."

Arawn was thoughtful. "You and I could post a letter to my cousin. With both Stewart and Tudor names as signatories, our concern might be heard. King Charles is not very well liked, as you know. Even if the King issued a proclamation that we desire, our efforts might be for naught if this civil war goes against our current King."

Three days later, Arawn and I posted a letter, sealed with the crests of both of our families. Life went on. As is common in times of war, both Sileas and Dolidh evidently had become pregnant while we were in hiding. The same was true of many in Cardigan. Andreas and Rebecca soon had several additional grandchildren. Sileas and I hired workers to enlarge our home again.

As the civil wars continued, skirmishes seemed to grow close from time to time, but the cave was utilized only twice more. Owena grew rapidly, and as she became a teenager, she grew into the role of a big sister to three younger brothers and two younger sisters.

I began to streak my hair with lemon juice. We did not yet share my story of the angel in the fire with our children. Sileas was wise enough to know, without my telling her, that our age difference was much greater than anyone realized. She decided that I was not sufficiently skilled to do a consistent job of streaking my hair. She made it our once-a-month shared ritual even as her hair was turning grey.

Baodan and Bethan were also getting older. We let them continue to do most of the work inside our now much larger home. I hired two more men to work our property outside, and I had a two-division cottage built to house them with their families. Soon we had both good crops to harvest and animals to sell.

On a warm June night in 1700, Sileas and I awakened because there was a subtle glow in our bedroom. We sat up and leaned against the headboard of our bed. The light did not come from the window, and everything was quiet because the rest of the family was sound asleep.

The glow took a human-like form. "The Lord is with you, Brianan and Sileas."

My wife's mouth was hanging open. "Who...?"

I put my arm around her. "I've seen this angel before, my love, a long time ago."

"Yes, Brianan, I first made myself known to you in the fire, but there shall be no fire this night."

"Why are you appearing to us?"

"Sileas Rees Tudor, you have been centered on your Lord Jesus all of your long life, and the Creator is pleased. Few months will pass before you return to the place prepared for you in heaven."

I shook my head. "She is still healthy. I need her here."

"In less than two years, she must return home. Already Andreas and Rebecca are waiting for her. As for you Brianan, you are almost ready for your next great adventure.

Considerably more will be required of you, and much additionally will be given to you."

Tears were running down my face. "I don't want to lose my Sileas."

"You are being told tonight so that you may prepare. You both belong to Jesus, and He is enough. There is yet much more to be accomplished. Our Father is pleased with both of you and loves you."

Quickly and silently the glow faded, and Sileas and I could see the first pink of dawn in the sky outside. Though it was earlier than usual, we rose and dressed. I went into my office, and Sileas went into the kitchen.

Later, during breakfast, Owena put her cup of tea down and spoke to us. "Mother, Father, Gareth has asked me to marry Him, and I have said yes." All of us around the table smiled and offered her congratulations. "Would it be too soon to have our wedding next month?"

I continued smiling. "Of course not! That will be wonderful! Your brother, Arthur, is marrying Adele in August, and we will expect all four of you – and later, your children – to live here at our estate. I know that Gareth does not have the means to purchase a home for you, so the two of you will make your home here, if he is willing."

Owena got up, came to me, and put her arms around me. "Oh, yes, I was hoping you would invite him!"

"Of course, Owena, your mother and I expected this. We are getting to the age when we need our children to help us run this estate. When your children come, if you want to build another house closer to the forest – or even on the bay – that will be perfectly fine."

Sileas nodded. "Your father and I have been planning for this for a long time."

What the angel had told us came to pass. In August of 1702, Sileas went home. Though I thought I was prepared for it, I was not. I became numb. I was married to Sileas more than twice as long as I was to Dearbhail. Suddenly not seeing her classic beauty was devastating. Her intelligence, her poise, her talents, and so much more were mixed in with a veritable flood of memories of the decades we were together.

I vaguely remember her funeral, with the church filled to overflowing. Hundreds of people joined us at her graveside, and

I spoke without thinking to all of those expressing their condolences. Arthur and Gareth joined me in walking home. The rest of that day, with the days that followed, are still a blur after all of these years. The wake lasted the rest of the day and long into the night.

It was after midnight when I went home and went to my bed. I cried myself to sleep. Sileas and I had been married over a half century. I felt an emptiness that cannot be put into words.

6.
Grief

Despite my preparations, for weeks, life seemed like a bad dream. I immersed myself in work to stave off my loneliness for short periods. All through our marriage, Sileas and I had read scriptures every morning and prayed. That early-morning time alone in my bed without Sileas became my anchor in life. Soon, I began praying more than I ever had.

Bishop Art had died several years earlier, and though I liked the new Vicar, Glyn, I did not find his counsel helpful. That added to my loneliness. Gradually, I came to realize that I had to leave Wales. Where would I go?

I sought out news from the latest Town Crier, Ian Morgan. I found him in the pub that Andreas had built many years earlier. I bought Ian a pint and invited him to sit with me.

As we walked towards a table, two men at the bar began to hurl insults at one another. "Bootless boil-brained bugbear!

"Fawning fen-sucked horn-beast!" It looked like the possible beginning of a brawl, but their friends kept them apart.

Ian and I sat down. "Tell me, Ian, what is the current news of the world beyond our beloved land?"

Ian took a big gulp of his ale. "Most of the news I hear is of our wars, with occasional bits of gossip from France and Bavaria." He paused. "Does news of those countries interest you, Brianan my friend?"

"Possibly, but there for a while, your predecessor gave me a good quantity of news about Jamestown."

He nodded. "Ah! News of the colonies comes to me now more frequently since our summer has begun. I understand that East Jersey and West Jersey are going to merge to form a colony called New Jersey, just south of New York."

I took a long swallow of my ale. "That sounds interesting. Is the governor of New York helping that to happen?"

He nodded. "That's what I understand."

"Thank you, Ian, you've given me much to think about."

"You're quite welcome, sir. Thanks for the ale."

In that moment, I knew what I was about to do. There were preparations to be made, and those would occupy my mind as I continued to deal with my grief over losing Sileas.

During that evening's family meal, I spoke to all of them. "I've decided that I need to get away from Cardigan for a while. I was talking with Crier Ian this afternoon, and I've decided that I want to visit the colonies, probably New York."

Owena put her fork down. "How long will you be gone?"

"I don't know. It will probably not be more than a year or two. I do not wish to sail in the winter, so I very likely will not return before the following summer." I turned to Arthur. "Last week, I learned that there are two ships sailing for the new world next week. I'm going to do my best to book passage. Tonight, Arthur, I want to talk with you before we retire for the evening."

He nodded. "Yes, Father."

That night, I told Arthur my full story from my mother's tryst with the King through the appearance of the angel in the flames. I gave Arthur the same instructions I had given to my first son, Ailean. Arthur took my hand. "Will we ever see you again, Father?"

"I honestly do not know, Arthur. I thought I would see my first son, Ailean, before now. I have not so much as caught a glimpse of him. Because of our wars, I am not even sure who of my first family is still alive. I am leaving it to you, Arthur, to pass on our family story at the right time, and do so accurately. I trust you to do that."

I said my farewells at the front of my estate early on a Monday morning. I hugged everyone. I also planted a kiss on my first grandson, born to Arthur and Adele a month earlier. Owena was very pregnant and due at any time. As Arthur drove me to the port, I had enough gold coins in a pocket for both my passage and some extra. Both my large trunk and a smaller one already was put in my cabin.

After hugging Arthur on the dock, I handed him a letter. "My son, wait a week before you open this. It tells you where to find your mother's diary that she kept, beginning on our wedding day and continuing until the evening before her death." I paused and took a deep breath. "Give your mother's diary to Owena, but don't read it unless Owena tells you that she wants you to. Furthermore, this letter tells you where to find my diary that I have kept, starting with the Sunday when I met your mother. God be with you, my son."

+ + +

I was one of eleven passengers on board the ship. Captain Griffith told us that our passage typically took ten to twelve days. The food was horrible, so I washed it down with ale most of the time. At first, we had fair sailing. On our fifth day, however, the ocean became rough as the wind began to blow. It was no small storm. The Captain passed the word to us that he was trying to find shelter in Iceland.

In the early afternoon of the sixth day, the rain had stopped, but there were still high seas due to the wind. The captain headed for Vestmannaeyjar, hoping to take refuge between the island and the mainland. As we got closer, the wind died down and the Atlantic seemed calmer. Suddenly, our ship lurched as we went aground. Our ship began to break up.

I vaguely remember seeing people on the shore waving their arms and shouting at us. I fell overboard. The next thing I knew, I was on a bed, covered with a rough woolen blanket. I smelled the aroma of tea. A young woman was standing beside the bed, looking down on me. In broken English, she asked if I would like some tea.

As I tried to sit up, I realized I was naked under the blanket. Somehow, I could sit on the edge of the bed, with the blanket around me. "Thank you," was all I managed to say at first. After a few sips of tea, I continued. "Where am I?"

"You're in Iceland. You have been sleeping for more than two days. Are you hungry?"

My stomach growled. "Yes, thank you."

As the young woman walked out, I saw my clothes neatly folded on a stool nearby, next to my two trunks. Quickly getting dressed, I went out the door. I found the girl with a man and woman seated around a table. The man indicated a chair for me. "Please sit down, Brianan. Do you remember what happened to you?"

Confusing images flitted through my mind. "The ship I was on was breaking up, and I fell overboard, and...."

"No, Brianan, that was last summer."

"Last summer...?"

Suddenly, many things came flooding over me. "You are Baldur and Mìa, and your daughter here is Hekla, and ... I was doing fine until I slipped on some ice. Was that two days ago?" I realized those were the two days of which she had spoken.

Hekla nodded vigorously. "Yes! I … we were worried about you!"

Baldur pointed at my plate. "Eat now. There will be no more ships coming here for at least three months."

As I ate, I remembered the situation. No one died. Everyone was staying with families here on the southern coast of Iceland. Most of the luggage – including both of my trunks – was saved. Since the shipwreck, I had been earning my keep by splitting wood and helping with other minor chores. Hekla had been pestering me for sex since we had celebrated the new year, but I was still grieving over Sileas.

Then, on a bright, sunny day in May of 1703, a ship dropped anchor nearby. As I helped unload deliveries, I touched the arm of one of the sailors. "Do you speak English?"

"Yes, sir, and your accent seems to say you are Welsh."

"That's right. Where are you going from here?"

"We will stop first at Boston, and then we will continue south to the other colonies. We have room for only one. If you want to go with us, we'll sail before sunset. You'd best get your belongings."

I was immensely pleased! "Thank God! I'll bring my trunks in a few minutes."

When I got back to the house, my hosts had loaded my two trunks onto their cart, and their donkey was hitched. I hugged each of them, and then I took Baldur aside. "You, your wife, and your daughter have been so kind to me." I reached into an inside pocket of my coat, and I handed him a small leather bag. "I think you'll be able to trade with these. I'm sorry that I cannot do more for you."

Baldur shook his head. "I cannot take this. You have been a friend to us as well."

I shook my head. "Please, Baldur, accept this as a token of my gratitude."

He accepted it, and as he loosened the drawstring to look inside, his eyes got bigger. "What is this? It is too much!"

"No, my friend, it is not. Please accept my gratitude." The four of us started walking behind the cart towards the shoreline. There, I hugged each of them again before getting into the launch boat.

+ + +

The captain of my second vessel identified himself simply as "the captain," and he wanted ten gold pieces for my remaining passage. It was too much, but I did not complain. He told me that my previous ship had been reported lost at sea. I decided that I would not try to correct that record.

Compared to the first part of my journey westward, sailing was quite smooth. After six days, we dropped anchor in the early afternoon in Boston's harbor. The ship would be there two days if I wanted to pay for further passage to the south.

At a shop near the harbor, I traded for some northeast coins that I had heard about. Then, after putting my belongings in a room at an inn, I began to explore the city. Boston was considerably larger than Cardigan, but I found it fairly easy to move around. Each morning I would read scriptures, pray, and cry quietly. In Iceland, I think it had been my tears that finally convinced Hekla that I was not good husband material.

I bought a small house just west of the main part of town, but I was restless. After a little more than a month, I sold it to a neighbor who wanted the land to grow more crops.

I liked Boston, but I was feeling lost. I bought a crude covered cart, and I started wandering southward. I tried keeping a diary, but because I could not focus very well, I burned the few pages I had written one night in my camp fire.

People were sociable. Sometimes I would stop and stay with a family for a few days, but there were no friendships that lasted because I kept moving. Almost always I was invited to go to church with them, and when the offering plate was passed, I would put in a gemstone or two – or three.

(This is one of the subtle miracles of my life. I always have a few of those gemstones somewhere. I've never run out of them. Each time I've thought I had run out, I would find another stash of them among my traveling effects.)

I constantly traveled further south, and did so very slowly. Summer was just beginning in 1776 when I traveled southward out of the colony of Georgia into the British colony of East Florida. It was terribly hot and humid. At the end of the summer, the town crier in Pensacola spread the news that war began in the thirteen colonies north of us. Despite the humidity, I liked the area. With plenty of cheap labor available, I built a home further west on the gulf, and I began to get my life put together again. There was a nice family that had property just east of me, and I enjoyed their friendship. Samuel, the husband, was a large and strong man, and he and I had a number of quiet conversations.

+ + +

A monumental storm took out all of my property with wind, rain, and an extremely high tide five years later. (Today we would call it a hurricane.) The family on the adjacent property lost everything but the clothing on their backs. We shared some food we could scavenge. Since they had not had as many life experiences as I had, they felt more lost than I did. In a quiet and private moment, I gave Samuel three gemstones, telling him that I had won them in a card game a few years earlier and did not want them anyway.

I left northwest Florida almost immediately and went even further west. I heard of a town called New Orleans, and that became my goal. My latest wagon was a little larger than the ones I had had previously.

I was disappointed in New Orleans, but I remained there for several years - almost ten. I could see no evidence of either laws or their enforcement. I spent most of my time in the *Vieux Carré*, or "Old Square" in English. In years to come, it would become known as the French Quarter. I took an apartment there, and I was reasonably comfortable.

One day, I got a letter. Postal markings indicated it had gone to New York, Boston, and several places down the Atlantic Seaboard. Evidently, my name was remembered in some of the towns I'd visited. The letter was from Arthur.

Dear Father,

I do not know if this letter will ever reach you. Three weeks after your ship sailed, we heard that all had been lost during a storm south of Iceland. I have been praying about it, and I believe you are still alive and in the New World. Believing this, I am writing this letter. It is now August of 1703. Mom went to heaven a year-ago yesterday.

As you may have discovered by now, I did not merely hide things in the smaller trunk, but in the larger one as well. I do not know if you will return to Cardigan, of course, but you may be safer where you are. The cave clan retreats less often, but these are unstable times. The families within the clan have created a food pantry in the basement of the chapel. Owena and Gareth organized it, and they supply food to nearly twenty needy families. You taught us well.

Adele and I, meanwhile, are taking food baskets to families too proud to go to the church to ask for help. We have five children. My beloved sister, who has seven children, decided early on with Gareth to pray with these families each time they received food. Adele and I are doing the same.

I know that you were not impressed with Vicar Glyn. Two months ago, in June, he told me that he sensed that about you, and he said he thought he knew why. He said that he was well aware that he was ineffective at public prayer. He also said that he was very impressed with your prayers. He asked me if you had taught me to pray as you did, and I said yes. After our first session with each other, he mentioned it to the congregation that Sunday morning. The second week, three more men joined us, and at present there are seven every week praying together. The lessons you gave me on prayer I've passed on to the other men.

Last Sunday, one of the grand-children of Ailean and Catir Thomas brought their baby to worship with a high fever. The seven of us prayed over her, and at the conclusion of worship, the fever had left her. Praise God!

Please know, Father, that whether or not you return to Cardigan, you have left a permanent mark on our community. Only Adele knows I'm sending this letter, and she sends her love. I've shared the family secret with her. I've also told Owena and Gareth.

Our love always,

Arthur

I read the letter several times before storing it in a safe place in my large trunk.

Prominent in New Orleans was the biggest river I had ever seen or had even imagined. I was told it was called the Mississippi. Bouncing from hotel to hotel for a while, I headed to the north side of town and built a home. I became a skilled trader, and when my honesty became well known, I developed many business friends. My business thrived, but, still grieving for Sileas somewhat, I became restless again.

In 1802, I said good-bye to my friends and headed north, up the river. After leaving the Florida territory, it took me several years to get up through the Mississippi, Tennessee, and Kentucky territories. Each time I met people and spent time with them, it slowed me down – thankfully. Slowly but surely, I began crying less.

When I entered into the Indiana territory, I met a man named Boone. He told me about a strange place where water was constantly boiling and shooting into the air. He also said that the air there smelled truly terrible.

This area is known as Yellowstone to this day, and I decided after days of praying about it that it was my next destination. I won't bore you with the details of the subsequent few years. Almost always, I was by myself. I was no longer thinking as much about Sileas. I was simply lonely. As I had been further south, I would spend some time working in a settlement for a few seasons, and then I would move on.

It was beginning to look like autumn when I entered a settlement named Fort Pierre Chouteau. At the trading post, I learned I would not be able to spend the winter out in the open without a sturdy and warm shelter. I was told about a boarding house, so I drove my wagon in that direction. The sun was going down, and it was getting very cold.

The proprietor had a room available, and I handed a gemstone to his wife. She said it would cover room and board for the winter. I agreed. After putting things in my room, I took my wagon to a barn and arranged care for my horses. As I was walking back, off on my left I noticed movement on the ground, and I walked over to investigate.

Lying on the ground was a woman with red hair. Her skin had a bluish cast. When I touched her forehead, she barely stirred. I never have figured out why I responded as fully as I did. I did not just want to help her. It seemed like I had to do more. Maybe her red hair reminded me of Sileas. The young woman seemed light like a feather as I picked her up and carried her to the boarding house.

"Who is that?" The owners' eyes were wide.

I shook my head. "I don't know. She was lying on the ground, like she was asleep, and she seems half frozen."

"We don't have room for another boarder."

"I'll take responsibility for her. I'll come down and make some tea for her in a few minutes."

Lucy, the wife, shook her head. "Tea? You're crazy! She needs hot chocolate and food! I'll bring it up in a few minutes!"

"Lucy!" Her husband sounded angry.

"You no never mind, Joe! I'm doing this!"

Joe shrugged his shoulders and went back into their room.

Lucy pointed upward. "At the end of the hall upstairs there's a closet. There you'll find an extra mattress and several blankets. She can sleep on the floor in your room."

I carried her upstairs and put her on my bed in my room while I got the other blankets and mattress. I took a night shirt out of one of my trunks, and after getting her mostly wet clothes off of her, I put her in a nightshirt, put her on the mattress on the floor, and put three blankets over her.

As I put one of my pillows under her head, she began to wake up. "Who... who are you? Where am I?" She tried to raise herself up but fell back down.

"My name is Brianan, and you're temporarily sharing my room here at the Johnson Boarding House in Pierre. Who are you?"

"I am Jacqueline DuPont. A man paid to bring me here from Paris, but when I got to New York, he was not there. I was told by one of his friends that I might be able to find him in Yellowstone." She stopped speaking as Lucy Johnson came in with a bowl of stew and hot chocolate.

"Thank you, but I have been robbed. I cannot pay you."

Lucy shook her head. "You're in Mr. Tudor's room, so he's paying for this, and I know he's good for it. Besides, I've been wanting to hire a maid to clean and help me cook. If you're interested, I'll put you to work." She paused because Jacqueline looked confused. "Don't worry about it now, dear. Get some sleep, and you'll feel better in the morning." She looked up at me. "Good might, Mr. Tudor. I knew you were a good man when we accepted you as a boarder." She went out quickly.

Jacqueline ate some more stew and swallowed. "Where did you find me?"

"I spotted you about fifty yards from here. I did not realize that the lump on the ground was a person until I got next to you. You were unconscious and starting to turn blue." I paused. "It sounds like you are a *femme à la poste* – a mail-order bride."

"Do you speak French?"

"I do not speak it well. I can get by if necessary." I pointed. "Your clothes are drying on top of that trunk, and there is a chamber pot behind that screen when you need it. Breakfast here is shortly after sunrise. I will lower the light now so we can both get some sleep."

"Thank you, Brianan. Is that name Irish?"

"No, it is Scots and Welsh. "Good night, Jacqueline."

"Good night."

+ + +

The winter passed slowly in Pierre. Jacqueline worked very hard as a maid and kept the entire rooming house truly clean. As it turned out, she was a much better cook than Lucy. Jacqueline introduced us to some marvelous French dishes made with our limited winter supplies.

About once a month, when the weather permitted, a boarder named John went hunting with Joe, and they brought back fresh meat. In February, John shot a six-point buck, and he and Joe quickly slaughtered it.

That evening, as all of us were feasting on venison steaks, I was thoroughly enjoying it. "This is the first time I've had venison for several years. It's great!" There were murmurs of agreement. "I have been carving a couple of spears in my spare time. How soon, Joe, will I be able to spear some fish for us in that big river?"

Joe chuckled. "That is the Missouri River. Are you any good at spearing fish?"

I smiled. "In Wales, it's a great sport, and I've done rather well."

"When we get a bright and sunny day, I'll grab my axe. I'll chop a hole through the ice, and you can try to spear us some. I'll be glad to help you bring them back and eat them."

Jacqueline drank some coffee. "When you clean them, don't cut off their heads and tails, just gut them. Lucy and I have already been talking about making a fish fry when we get some."

Five days later, the day started with no clouds in the sky. Lucy and Jacqueline stayed in the house, but the rest of the boarders joined Joe and I for our fishing party. Joe had a couple of long, rough-hewn boards for us to put across the ice for us. The others built a fire on the shore.

It did not take long to chop a hole through the ice. The sun was fairly high in the sky when I picked up a spear and looked down through the hole. I was surprised at how very clear the water was. "Joe, how big do they get?"

"Three years ago, I brought one in that was nearly two feet long, but most of what I've caught have been twelve to fifteen inches."

When I threw the spear the first time, I was glad I had a long leather thong connecting it to my wrist. I almost lost the spear. After a short struggle, I hauled it in, and Joe bludgeoned it. He held the head next to his knee, and its tail just touched the ice. "It looks to be about fifteen inches, Brianan. I guess you weren't just braggin' when you said you could spear some fish."

I was able to spear eight more that were about that length, and I got six that were slightly shorter. Most of them were bass, with a few walleye. It was late afternoon when we went back to the house. It was wonderfully warm inside.

Jacqueline took the big leather creel into the kitchen. As Lucy took the fish out, she practically shouted her delight. "My land, that Brianan of ours is quite a fisherman! We've enough here for a real Missouri River fish deal. Start putting buffalo grease on a sheet of wrapping paper, Jacqueline."

"Let's wrap each fish separately and use plenty of salt and pepper."

Lucy shook her head. "We're running low on pepper, and I want it for fixing eggs. I've ground some sage. Let's use that. It's hot in here because I've got the oven fired up as hot as it will go."

"Bien!"

Though that dinner was about two hundred fifty years ago, in my memory I can still taste that bass baked with buffalo grease, salt, and sage. I suppose that in the twenty-first century, bacon grease might serve almost as well.

During those long winter months, I helped Jacqueline learn better English, and she taught me about European history I hadn't learned in Scotland. Having learned that I was headed towards Yellowstone, she asked if she could travel with me, and I agreed. We became fast friends. In the Spring, I procured a covered wagon, and in mid-May, we said our good-byes to Joe and Lucy as we headed west.

We had been traveling for about two weeks when we were approached by Shoshone Indians, which we now call Native Americans, of course. That was the first time I discovered the gift that I didn't previously know I had. As Jacqueline and I tried to communicate with them, I was listening carefully to what they said to one another as well as to us. Suddenly, I grasped their language.

"You call yourselves Shoshone? We have heard about your wonderful people."

Their leader grunted and stared at me.

"You have a beautiful language. I find it nice to learn."

"Good, where are you going?"

"We are seeking a place of boiling pools and strong smells called Yellowstone."

He grunted. "Yes. I was there once. You will reach it before the skies begin to turn dark and cold."

I nodded. "Thank you, that is good to know."

I turned to Jacqueline. "Their language is beautiful and easy to learn. They are Shoshones. If they invite us to join them for a meal, we should probably do so."

She nodded. "Okay."

We had a meal with all of them. I shared some venison I had previously salted, and they shared fish with us. They were a hunting party, and they traveled with us three days before turning back.

In the middle of August, it was scorching hot when, in the distance, we got our first glimpse of Lake Yellowstone. Jacqueline pointed. "There! That lake is huge!"

I nodded. "I think we will reach it tomorrow. We'll have to stop for the night soon."

Arriving at the lake, we soon came upon a cabin. There was smoke coming from the chimney. A woman about Jacqueline's age came out to greet us. "Hello! Welcome! We do not get very many visitors here! I am Sandra Smith."

We got down from our wagon, and Jacqueline went up to take the woman's hand. "Did you say your name is Sandra Smith?"

"Yes, why, are you looking for someone?"

"I know that Smith is a fairly common name, but do you happen to know a Hank Smith?"

Sandra nodded. "That is my husband's name. He sent for a bride from France, but her ship was lost at sea. I met him in St. Louis last year, and we got married."

Jacqueline was very quiet until we left about an hour later.

7.
Further West

"I am so very sorry, Jacqueline." She was riding with me in front, and we had ridden silently several miles north and away from the man she had been engaged to.

"I'm glad he returned to join his wife before we left. At least, I got to meet the man who paid for my passage to this country. I could not tell him who I was, and I'm glad you did not tell him." She put her arm around my shoulders and hugged me. "Where are we going now?"

"Hank said that he heard there is civil war coming. I experienced civil war in Scotland, and I don't have the stomach for war right now. I think we should go around the north side of the lake, and then go on westward across the mountains. Is that okay with you?"

"Yes, it is okay, Brianan. I want to continue with you, if you don't mind."

I nodded. We rode silently the rest of the day.

After we ate that evening, we sat on the ground next to the dying embers of our cooking fire. "Brianan, I need to ask you something." She stared at the fire.

She paused, and I remained silent. I was pretty sure of what she wanted to discuss, but I had to let her tell it.

"Brianan, I am thousands of miles from my home and family. So are you. Out here, we have no friends but each other. Would you please consider, at least until we get wherever we're going, whether or not you would like to have me as your wife?"

It had been more than hundred and fifty years since Sileas died in 1702. I had realized that I had stopped grieving when I was fishing in that hole through the ice. I cleared my throat and spoke carefully. "Just before I left Scotland, my wife died." I touched Jacqueline's hand. "I grieved for her for a long time. Her name was Sileas. I put my children in the hands of relatives and friends, and I took an ocean voyage to try to forget." All of this was basically true, of course, and I let Jacqueline assume the rest for her time frame.

"I have been very interested in you from the beginning, but since you were engaged to a man out west, I have kept my lust for you under control. Since you have been reading the Bible with me for a long time, you know I am a Christian gentleman." I touched her hand again. "Ever since we drove our wagon away from that cabin this morning, I have been considering the future. Your question is a beautiful solution to my struggle. Yes, Jacqueline, I will be honored to have you as my wife."

She hugged me, and then she kissed me on my cheek. "Do you think we will be able to find a clergyman out here?"

I shook my head. "I do not think we will be able to find a member of the clergy, unless we go into a large settlement like San Francisco." I paused. "Still, if God hears us say our vows to one another, will that be enough for you?"

"*Certainement*! Certainly!"

That evening, we sat inside the wagon, drinking the remainder of the coffee left over from our meal. I prayed, and then got out my Geneva Bible and read the thirteenth chapter of the Apostle Paul's first letter to the people of Corinth. Next, I looked into Jacqueline's eyes. "I'm going to try to duplicate the vows I've heard so many times. Just repeat after me, but where I say my name, you say yours, and vice versa. Where I say 'husband' you say 'wife' and conversely. Do you understand?"

She nodded.

"I, Brianan Tudor, take you, Jacqueline Dupont, to be my wedded wife."

"I, Jacqueline Dupont, take you, Brianan Tudor, to be my wedded husband."

"I now covenant with God and with you to be your wedded husband."

"I now covenant with God and with you to be your wedded wife."

"I will worship with you and read scriptures with you, Jacqueline."

"I will worship with you and read scriptures with you, Brianan."

"I will pray with you and pray for you, Jacqueline."

"I will pray with you and pray for you, Brianan."

"Jacqueline, I will do these things, whether in abundance or in want, and whether in sickness or in health."

"Brianan, I will do these things, whether in abundance or in want, and whether in sickness or in health."

"I will love you unconditionally and trust you unconditionally, Jacqueline, as long as we both shall live."

"I will love you unconditionally and trust you unconditionally, Brianan, as long as we both shall live."

We kissed for the very first time, and that night, we became one.

We continued southward the next day to a settlement called Jackson, where we found a Protestant clergyman. His name was Steven Jones. "I'm impressed that you worshiped and said your vows before considering yourself married. So many people here in the west don't bother with those formalities."

"We're both Christians."

"This is excellent. I will record your marriage in my records here at the chapel, and I will file a copy with the settlement's records at the bank. Where are you headed?"

I lowered my voice slightly, because there were others at the rear of the chapel. "We understand that we have a new President named Abraham Lincoln, and that our country is plunging into civil war. We are headed toward the Presidio area of San Francisco. Having seen war in Scotland, I have no stomach for it."

Pastor Jones nodded. "Since autumn will soon be here, I suggest you work your way more southward than westward for a while. A group called Mormons have a large settlement at the Great Salt Lake. You two may want to spend the winter there. Then, in the Spring, before it gets too hot, cross the desert from there westward towards San Francisco. You will have to traverse a mountain range before going towards the San Francisco Bay."

I nodded. "Evidently, you have seen all of this, have you?"

He nodded. "My parents were missionaries, and I was born in San Juan Bautista. When I became a teenager, I decided I wanted to go east and see New York. I haven't made it yet because I was needed here in Jackson, and I've gotten married. I don't know whether we will ever see New York and Boston."

Before leaving Jackson, Jacqueline and I found a hotel that advertised the availability of a bathtub. We took advantage of the opportunity and spent the night before setting out southward.

It was three weeks before we saw our first glimpse of the Great Salt Lake. Jacqueline was beginning to show the outward signs of being pregnant, so we did not rush our traveling. As we pulled into the large settlement that had been established by the Mormon group, we were glad pastor Steven had suggested we spend the winter there. We made several new friends, including a doctor, as Jacqueline began to deal with the final month of having our first child.

It was a boy. For my own selfish reasons, I wanted to name him Arthur, but Jacqueline prevailed over me with the name James. Her father's name was Jacques. She wrote a long letter to her family in France, and it was posted to go on the next train eastbound.

After Easter of the Spring of 1861, we decided that we must continue westward. News of the civil war seemed to be getting closer, and we both longed for our little family to be safe. Traveling to avoid war was so very different than hiding out in that cave in Wales! As we crossed over the Sierra Nevada mountains, I told Jacqueline that I was getting concerned because I had only a few more gemstones in the little pouch that I carried in my right boot. One evening, after nursing James and putting him to sleep, she searched my trunks, which were battered and worn from so many years of travel. Jacqueline found a hidden compartment near the bottom of my largest trunk – a compartment I had forgotten about. In it were two more pouches of gemstones. God is so good!

We continued west, and some of the traveling was difficult. Jacqueline and I would trade with a gemstone or two when we needed supplies. The summer heat was like none either of us had ever experienced. It was the last day of August when we reached the Presidio of San Francisco. During the month of September, there were clear blue skies and pleasant breezes. At the end of the first week of October, we began to find out what most of the weather in San Francisco is really like. It was cold and wet.

Neither Jacqueline nor James liked San Francisco, but we lived there three years. Jacqueline got pregnant again. I began to develop acquaintances in the Chinese community. It took me nearly two months before I could speak Mandarin Chinese fluently. I could easily see that my gift was going to become very profitable.

After Anne was born, Jacqueline and I talked about moving further south, but instead we moved to the east side of the bay. There, we made new friends. We built a little home among the hills there, facing west. We hardly ever had any fog, which was a relief to everyone but me. Since I had come from Scotland, the fog of San Francisco had not bothered me.

Shortly after moving into our new home, one of my Chinese clients in San Francisco had a messenger bring a letter to me. The original postmark was Fort Pierre, South Dakota. Attached to it was a note from a Chinese merchant friend named Chao Lee. "Brianan, I'm sorry, but this accidentally went to China, and it came to me yesterday."

> Brianan,
>
> I'm sending this to Yellowstone. If you're not there, I hope it will get to Jacqueline, and that she can send it on to you.
>
> We are so glad you spent that winter with us. Lucy and I have started going to worship services every Sunday. She said that she had never taken God seriously until you came. She's sending you a letter in the same mail pouch as this one. She's telling you all kinds of things in her letter that I don't need to. God bless you!
>
> Joe

I shared the letter with Jacqueline. After reading it, she smiled. "This is really like Joe! I wonder if we'll ever get Lucy's letter?"

I shook my head. "This one went to China before getting here. It seems unlikely we'll ever hear from Lucy."

We were shopping in the ever-growing settlement on the east side of the bay one day, and we went into a restaurant to eat. The owner's name was Dave, and his wife's name was Maria. They had five children who were trying their best to help with the business but frequently made messes instead.

Jacqueline touched Maria's arm. "Do you and your husband ever get any time away from your business, just for yourselves and your children?"

She shook her head. "All of our friends are business-related. The waiters and waitresses are like family, and so are the cooks. Dave and I can leave them in charge when we have to go shopping, but we seldom do more than that. Where do you and Brianan live?"

I smiled and nodded at Jacqueline, and she responded. "We have a house up on one of the hills and facing the ocean." She paused. "Our kids seem to like your kids. If you and Dave would like to spend a day with us, the kids could play outside around the house."

Maria smiled. "That would be wonderful. I'll talk to Dave today, and we'll decide on a day." She paused. "What do you do, sir?"

"Before we were married, I discovered that I have a gift. I can listen to people talking in another language, and in a short time, I can begin talking with them. It's amazing. I often can't write in those other languages, but I can speak them." (By then, I had confidence in speaking of the gift.)

Maria was thoughtful. "My native tongue is Spanish, so I speak it as well as I speak English."

Jacqueline nodded. "Before we moved to this side of the bay, Brianan acted as a translator for some of the Chinese businessmen there on the other side of the bay. There are Chinese moving to this side of the bay now, so he will probably have to do more of that again. He's fairly fluent in Spanish, and he's also conversant in French because I taught him as we traveled."

I smiled. "There's a strong Chinese culture throughout the bay area." I paused. "If you and Dave want to bring the kids to our house on Thursday, my day is fairly free that day."

Jacqueline and I welcomed that family to our home that Thursday. It was the beginning of friendship that would last until the earthquake of 1906. It turned out that Dave and I had mutual interests in hunting and fishing. Jacqueline and Maria both loved cooking and baking, and Jacqueline began to help out in the restaurant's kitchen from time to time. She introduced some French dishes to Maria and the restaurant. Our kids got along famously. Eventually, our oldest son, James, would marry one of their daughters, Mary.

On James' thirteenth birthday, he asked if we could travel to the Sierras and see some of the Sequoia trees that he read about. Dave and Maria Kennedy had never taken a vacation, and Jacqueline and I also needed a change of pace. Our families agreed to take the month of May for travel to the Sierras. It was the last quarter of the nineteenth century, and everything in California was growing rapidly.

With so many of us traveling together, we could not take a stage coach, so we rode trains as far as a community called Modesto. There we got a large wagon and headed into the mountains. According to a Chinese businessman I had talked to, the nearest grove of Sequoias was called the Tuolumne Grove. The days were getting considerably longer, so we reached the grove in three days.

Jacqueline fell in love with the trees, and the rest of us were nearly overwhelmed with their size. "James! Happy Birthday again! This is a gift for all of us!"

Our son grinned. "Aren't they great?"

Nearby, a carriage stopped, and a distinguished-looking couple stepped out. Jacqueline pointed. "I met that woman a long time ago, when I first arrived in this country. At that time, her name was Jane Lathrop. I've seen pictures of that man with her in the newspaper, but I don't remember his name."

"Let's talk with them." Dave and Maria followed discretely behind us as I took Jacqueline's arm. We approached the couple. "Good afternoon!"

When the couple acknowledged our greeting, Jacqueline spoke with the woman. "You may not remember me, but we met when we were much younger. Are you not Jane Lathrop?"

The woman blinked twice, and her eyes grew large. "Jacqueline Dupont! It has been a long time! This is my husband, Leland Stanford."

Jacqueline curtsied and smiled. "Good afternoon, sir! This is my husband, Brianan Tudor."

Leland Stanford shook my hand. "Brianan Tudor? It is good to meet you. Aren't you the linguist who lives in Oakland?"

I nodded. "It is I. It seems I heard you speak two years ago, at the south end of the bay in a community known as San Jose. As I recall, you are in the mercantile business, and are also building railroads." I turned slightly. "These are our friends, Dave and Maria Kennedy. They have a restaurant in Oakland."

The six of us began to stroll among the giant Sequoias, and our children kept their distance. "I see that you have several children." Leland spoke quietly. "Jane and I have but one son. He did not come with us on this trip. Tudor is a Scots-Irish name, is it not?"

I nodded. "Although my family comes from royalty, I left all that behind when I sailed into Boston some years past."

"Since you're a linguist, by any chance do you speak Chinese?"

"I speak Mandarin Chinese with fair fluency. A businessman I know in San Francisco is bringing in laborers from China to help build railroads. Is that why you ask?"

Stanford nodded. "Yes. Perhaps the next time I am negotiating for labor I will call upon you."

We walked among the Sequoias with them for more than two hours before they returned to their carriage and drove away. After making camp, our families spent more than a week there before taking the wagon back to the train station. We were away from Oakland and the restaurant for 29 days, and Dave and Maria were pleased to see that the restaurant had thrived without them.

The next day, our vacation was behind us. Jacqueline helped at the restaurant, and I began to get calls as a translator. Life was good.

About a year passed, and then Leland Stanford asked me to listen in on contract negotiations for labor. Most of the negotiations were in English, but periodically the Chinese negotiator turned to friends and spoke in Mandarin Chinese. When we would stop for coffee, I would quietly fill him in on what had been said.

Time seemed to fly by more quickly. I was well established as a linguist, and several times I was invited to get into politics. I knew that was not what God wanted. As Jacqueline and I saw our children get married and move out, she and I considered moving into the San Francisco Presidio area again. We prayed about it for weeks. Finally, we decided that we would stay in Oakland.

Before telling James the family story and family secret, I told Jacqueline one night, after we had gone to bed. After I finished the story, she cocked her head to one side and studied me carefully. "I have been wondering when you would tell me. I decided right after James was born that I would let you tell me when you were ready."

I was shocked. "After James was born?"

She nodded. "I had my suspicions as we were traveling towards Yellowstone, but I decided not to say anything for fear that I was wrong, and you would think me crazy. When you first looked at James after he was born, suddenly, somehow I knew."

"I sure do love you, Jacqueline."

"And I love you too. Do you think I should start putting streaks of grey into your hair?"

I smiled and nodded.

With the family secret firmly in my beloved Jacqueline's consciousness as well as mine, we began to plan for the future in greater detail. She wanted to make the most of our remaining time together, and so did I. One time, during our conversation just before sleeping, she asked about Dearbhail and Sileas, and my feelings after their deaths. On another occasion, after we prayed with each other, she wanted to talk about her eventual death and how it would impact our children. We prayed about it together.

Many evenings, Jacqueline and I snuggled in front of a fire and talked about train travel to the east, but we always decided not to leave Oakland. "Leland Stanford's railroad lines are being established throughout the state, and California is now connected with the rest of the country via these rail lines."

She smiled. "Stanford gave you that letter of introduction that we have carried with us whenever we do train travel. The letter got us free fare or a discount throughout our train travels in the state."

"Jane probably suggested that to him because of your long friendship with her."

She looked up at me. "You're probably right. That letter has meant that frequently you have taken me with you when you have had to travel out of the area. Soon we'll begin a new century. I wonder how many more times we can use that letter?"

+ + +

The approaching new century meant that newspapers and magazines engaged in many months of anticipation. There were reviews of the century as well as projections of the coming decades. In Dave and Maria's restaurant, the table talk was frequently about the forthcoming celebrations of the New Year and new century. It meant improved business for them as people lingered over dessert to talk about it.

Many books were written, both fiction and non-fiction, about what seemed to lie ahead. Since the children had moved out, Jacqueline was beginning to slow down. Dave and Maria joined us almost every week for outings to various places.

We particularly enjoyed visiting the wineries. Although in California's early years, most wine was produced within the Los Angeles area, the gold rush prior to the Civil War shifted the majority of commercial wine production to Northern California. Jacqueline particularly enjoyed visiting the vineyards north of San Francisco.

As the end of the year finally approached, there was a mixture of both excitement and possible panic. Still, there was surprising excitement about the Pan-American Exposition that was being prepared in Buffalo, New York, to be operational throughout 1901. Jacqueline and I decided to take the train there during the summer. We asked Dave and Maria to join us one morning, when we were having breakfast at their restaurant. Dave shook his head. "We would have to be gone at least a month, possibly two. I don't see how we can be away from here that long."

Maria smiled. "Dave! It would be a real vacation. The children know how to run the place, for heaven's sake! We can afford it! Besides, we've not taken a real vacation since that trip, years ago, to the Sequoia Grove in the Sierras. Let's go!"

Jacqueline looked at him. "Yes, Dave, we'd love to have you and Maria go with us. Up until now, Brianan and I haven't wanted to travel that far east, but this Pan-American Exposition should be truly exciting!"

Dave was thoughtful, and then he looked straight at Maria and nodded. "We can go in a sleeper car, with adjacent rooms. I think they call those cars 'Pullmans.' You and I can have a second honeymoon, Maria!"

Maria hugged him and kissed him.

When Jacqueline and I got back home that evening, Jacqueline picked up our phone and asked the operator to help her call the widow of Leland Stanford. "Good evening, Jane, this is Jacqueline."

"Jacqueline! It is so nice to hear from you. I haven't heard from you or Brianan since Leland's funeral."

"Yes, Jane, that was a sad day. How are you doing?"

"Actually, I hardly have the time to think about how much I miss him. I keep myself immersed in the University named for our deceased son. How are you and Brianan?"

"We're doing quite well. You probably remember Dave and Maria Kennedy, the restaurant owners that were with us when we all met in that Sequoia Grove."

"Yes, I remember them as being very warm and friendly. Your children all played well together."

"Yes, they did! We have been talking about going to the Pan-American Exposition in the summer of 1901. The Kennedys are going to join Brianan and me, and we want to travel by Pullman Car. If you still have an active knowledge of the railroads, I'm wondering if you can recommend how we should travel there."

"What are friends for? I can set it up for you! When do you want to leave?"

Talking on the phone, Jane couldn't see Jacqueline smile. "We want to leave the first week in June."

"Excellent! The days will be long and enjoyable. You'll probably want to stay in Buffalo at least two weeks, but I'll arrange for you to be able to return whenever you decide to. Do you and Brianan still have the same phone in Oakland?"

"We do."

"Good, I'll call you no later than Friday evening, Wednesday evening at the earliest. I'll talk to you then, Jacqueline. Bye!"

"Thank you, Jane, good-bye!"

Jane was as good as her word. The train tickets and hotel reservations came by messenger less than two weeks later. At first, Jane talked about going with us in another compartment of the same Pullman Car, but then she realized that she had to be on the campus of the university at graduation time.

On New Year's Eve, Jacqueline and I helped out Dave and Maria at their restaurant. Between six and midnight, there was one price for the night, with meals including wine or beer. It was packed, and everyone had a good time. After midnight, most of the people began going home. Dave and Maria went upstairs to their apartment, and their kids ran the restaurant the rest of the night. Jacqueline and I went home.

The next seventeen months were mostly uneventful, except that on the first day of March, our second grandchild was born to James and Mary. Jacqueline and I began packing a steamer trunk and two suitcases for our trip to Buffalo. My largest antique trunk, which I had brought from Wales, was still fully functional, although it was showing the scars of time. On

Tuesday, June 4, we got on the train with the Kennedys. We were looking forward to being gone for most of the summer.

Originally, the Exposition was supposed to have been held on Cayuga Island, which is near Niagara Falls. The organizers thought tourists could take in both attractions. Those plans were set aside when the Spanish-American War broke out. Organizers considered both Niagara Falls and Buffalo, but Buffalo won because it was bigger and had better railroad connections. The Exposition was lit by power generated at Niagara Falls, about twenty-five miles away.

The most prominent attractions were the Electric Tower designed by John Galen Howard, and the Electricity Building that promoted various technology pieces that used the new alternating current. Jacqueline and Maria were particularly taken with the "Temple of Music" concert hall. Dave and I spent many hours in the Mines, Forestry, and Graphic Arts Building. We spent nearly three weeks there.

Although our train had taken us to Buffalo through northern states, coming back we first went down the Atlantic coast to Atlanta and changed trains to go west. When we reached Los Angeles, we took our final leg home going north.

As our train was approaching Oakland on the fourth of September, Jacqueline sighed. "This has been an amazing summer, and this has been a trip of a lifetime." She turned to me. "The only thing that can compare to this summer, was the journey you and I made together, starting in South Dakota."

I gave her a light kiss. "We'll not forget that, and our children won't either. We've seen to that."

Dave looked out the window. "There's been one strange thing for me."

"What's that?" I smiled.

"Our restaurant was on my mind until we got to Buffalo, and then I never gave it another thought until a few moments ago." He looked at Maria. "Does that surprise you, dear?"

She shook her head. "I put the restaurant out of my head about halfway across the country. When I saw our favorite winery about an hour ago, as we passed by, I thought of our work again. It was good to get away, Dave."

Two days later, we were eating a late dinner together when we read terrible news in the Oakland Tribune. Jacqueline had opened the latest issue while our coffee cups were being refilled. "Oh, my! President McKinley has been shot!"

I was dumbfounded, and so were Maria and Dave. I shook my head. "I'm glad we left Buffalo before that happened!"

The others nodded. As we ate our dessert, we did not feel like talking. The aftermath of the assassination filled the newspapers for weeks afterward.

+ + +

Four and a half years passed. On April 18, 1906, shortly after 5:00 AM, Dave and Maria were in the walk-in refrigerator at their restaurant, when the ground began to move. The walls of the refrigerator were not merely insulated. They were heavily framed, and the two of them had only minor bruises from things falling on them.

When the ground began to move under our house in Oakland's hills, I was in our bathroom, shaving, and Jacqueline was still in bed. I was barely able to stay on my feet. Our bed rolled across the bedroom, crashing into the farthest wall. That wall, along with the ceiling, crashed on top of her. I was able to crawl out of a hole in our roof, but I was not able to see Jacqueline's body for several hours.

You might think that, having lived as long as I had by that time, 317 years, that Jacqueline's death was easier on me than the first two. It wasn't. I vaguely remember digging a hole in the yard to bury her. There was no one to help, and I would have refused help if it had been offered. Decades later, Samantha's mother told me that there was a cemetery on that hill about where the house must have been. Jacqueline's body was the first resident.

8.
The Grand Canyon

Although the house that Jacqueline and I had built was mostly destroyed, our children's houses fared rather well. James and Mary invited me to stay with them, and I agreed. After I had been with them about a week, James and I talked one evening about what was left of the house up on the hill. James had tears in his eyes. "I grew up there, Dad, so that house has – had - special meaning for me. I want to salvage whatever else we can, and then I want to remove the debris and plant some shrubs."

I nodded. "I've been thinking along similar lines. There is a statuary place over on North Broadway. I want to order something for your mother's grave."

"Can I go with you?"

"Of course!"

Both of us were surprised at how many things Jacqueline had saved. It took a long time to work through the rubble. We took everything salvageable back to James' house, and at Thanksgiving, a couple of months later, we divided everything up among the children and their families. I worked almost every day, getting rid of debris, and landscaping the property. James helped me on weekends and on some evenings. The monument that James and I ordered was small enough to be mostly hidden by foliage. Hikers might stumble upon it, but it was not likely.

For a year, I avoided working as much as possible. I walked many miles, all over the San Francisco Bay area. On Easter Sunday of 1907, the family was together for dinner after church. Most of them belonged to First Christian Church on Fairmount Avenue, which was less than a mile from where I was living with James and Mary.

As we were eating, James made an announcement. "Mary and I want to trace the roots of the Tudors in the British Isles and the Duponts in France. We've booked passage for our family on a steamer leaving the fifteenth of June from New York, which means we'll take the train from Oakland to New York in

May. Does anyone else in the family want to go with us?" We discussed it throughout the dinner. No one else felt that they could go.

As we were eating our apple-pie dessert, I too made an announcement. "Last month, I got a letter from an old friend who is an executive with the Union Pacific Railroad." I took a forkful of pie, chewed, and swallowed, and drank some coffee. "His name is Jack Cody. He tells me that there is a town growing out in the desert called Las Vegas. He says that the railroad could use a linguist to help communicate with the variety of people both living in the area and passing through. I've decided to go down there and investigate."

When I took James, Mary, and their two children to the railroad station in May, I also was packed and ready for another train. I was headed south to Los Angeles, and then I would travel east to Las Vegas. Although I had prayed extensively about that journey, I was totally unprepared for what I found when I arrived.

The little town covered slightly over a hundred acres, and it was as though I had gone fifty years backward in time. Although Nevada had become a state in 1864, the settlement was rustic and nearly primitive in appearance. I soon discovered that virtually everyone spoke English, and I had very little work to do as a linguist, even in the most popular gambling establishments. The railroad had misjudged the population considerably.

On a hot August night, I listened in on a conversation about some beautiful canyons that were east and south of town. One of the canyons, called Zion, was being discussed in Washington, D.C., about becoming a national monument. In the 1850s, a settler named Isaac Behunin supposedly named the canyon "Zion" after a Biblical reference. It sounded interesting to me.

Another canyon nearby, was said to be very different. It was not much of a canyon, the story teller said, but it was very red and colorful. He said his great-grandfather, Ebenezer Bryce, had named the place Bryce Canyon because it was part of his Mormon homestead.

As I listened, I began to get sleepy because, even in that heat, I would eventually have to get some sleep. Suddenly, I was wide awake. Someone mentioned the Grand Canyon. The story-teller said that it would probably become a national monument the next year. He said that the canyon was approximately three hundred miles long and almost twenty miles wide in places. He also said that it was a mile deep in places. I had heard of the Grand Canyon, but I had not realized that it was so big. Wide awake again, I listened intently for another hour.

The next morning, I went into the railroad station to visit with my friend who had brought me to Las Vegas, Jack Cody. I walked into his office and shook his hand. "Good morning, Jack. Am I disturbing you?"

"No, not at all. What can I do for you, Brianan?"

"Jack, as I said a couple of months ago, I think the railroad seriously miscalculated in thinking that it could use the services of a linguist. In the last three weeks, I've only had one occasion when I was needed."

Jack nodded. "I understand. What do you want to do?"

"You originally said that I should give it at least a year, but that was before we had an accurate assessment of the situation. I suggest that we give this experiment until Christmas. I don't mind collecting a regular paycheck, whether I work or not, but if I'm not earning my pay by Christmas, I think I should move on."

Jack was thoughtful. He nodded. "I'll agree with you, Brianan. We'll talk about it again on Christmas."

That night, I prayed about it through the night. When I awakened, I knew that I would be moving on right after Christmas.

+ + +

On the day-after Christmas, I got on to a train going east, with a ticket to St. George, Utah. After obtaining lodging in a rooming house, I left most of my belongings there and rode in a truck with a few others into Zion Canyon. As beautiful as it was, I knew that I could not stay there, so after a week I took a bus to Bryce Canyon.

In hindsight, I was searching for something, but at the time, I was not sure just for what I was searching. I wandered about in Bryce Canyon for a couple of weeks. The more I wandered, the more lost I felt.

I went back to St. George, and I found Pine Valley Church just north of town. Time flew by. I worshiped there on Sundays, and I prayed there frequently during the week. In many conversations with people, one place constantly came up for discussion: Lee's Ferry. The calendar said that it was April of 1912.

I found a truck going to various stops to the east, and ending at Lee's Ferry. I talked with the driver about his work. "I understand you're Sam Laughton, and you're headed east, making deliveries, ending up at Lee's Ferry. Could you use some extra muscle to help you make those deliveries?"

Sam looked at me up and down. "I might. What's your name?"

"I'm Brianan Tudor. I'm hoping my belongings will fit on the truck. I have only one trunk and a suitcase. I'm a hard worker and an honorable Christian gentleman."

"You're a Christian, huh? Are you a Mormon?"

"No, sir, I'm just a Jesus follower who reads his Bible."

He cocked his head. "Okay. We'll leave tomorrow morning at dawn. Bring your stuff."

I worked very hard for the next two and a half weeks. At night, my muscles often ached more than they had when I was a young fisherman in Scotland. As it turned out, Sam made deliveries throughout southern Utah, southern Nevada, and northern Arizona. He knew every road and every town. He had a good one-man business, and he was popular with his customers.

After we unloaded the last of our cargo at Lee's Ferry, Sam and I sat down to eat some sandwiches. He swallowed a bite and looked at me. "Brianan, I've taken to likin' you. You're a hard worker. I'm picking up westward-bound shipments here. I'll be staying north of the big ditch, taking supplies to small burgs as I go. I'll be going as high as a settlement around a pond called Jacob Lake, and afterwards I'll continue west and down into the desert to Pipe Spring. Later, I'll complete the loop and go back to St. George. I could use your help. What do you think?"

I finished a sandwich before responding. "If I go with you, will we be seeing much of the canyon?"

He chewed and thought for a minute. "I'll tell you what. A friend of mine named Bill Wylie is starting to set up a settlement in a place on the north rim of the canyon called Bright Angel Point. I know he needs some supplies. I can pick them up for him right here at Lee's and deliver them to him. That'll give us a good view of part of the big ditch."

I nodded. "That sounds good." I paused, feeling as though God or His angel was giving me a nudge. "Yes." I nodded again. "I think that's a place I need to see."

We finished our lunch, and then we loaded up the supplies that Sam had mentioned. It was a tight fit, but we shifted some of the other cargo to make room.

It was totally dark, with less than a half-moon, when Sam said we were almost there. I was glad that he knew where he was going. It was a dirt road, and it was fairly rough. As we came into Wylie Way Camp, they had seen us coming. A man was waiting beside Sam's truck door when he opened it. "Hey, Sam, this is a great surprise! Did you bring us anything?"

Sam nodded. "I sure did. You told me last month what you were short of, so I brought you a pretty good supply."

"Great! I've got some messages for you. Who's this?" The man pointed at me.

"This is Brianan Tudor. He's been my extra muscle since I left St. George a month ago. Brianan, this is Bill Wylie."

I shook his hand. "It's good to meet you. I told Sam I wanted to see his big ditch, and this is the result."

Bill nodded. "You won't see much tonight, but if you're up at sunrise, you're bound to see one of the most beautiful sights on Earth."

We talked through the night. Sam and I had several helpings of venison stew. Bill repeatedly expressed his appreciation for the supplies we had brought to him.

The next morning I got up with the first pre-dawn glow. Watching the sunrise, I kept reminding myself that it was not a dream.

I prayed. I told God that I hoped that Dearbhail, Sileas, and Jacqueline could see through my eyes. As I look back now, after many years, I think that my grief began to subside into the background of my life from that moment, when the first rays of sunlight came across from the horizon.

After spending two nights there, Sam and I began working our way west on mostly dirt roads. As we were at higher altitude, the work seemed harder than it had between St. George and Lee's Ferry. We slept two nights in the truck. It was cold! Then towards evening after a long day, we stopped near what was either a very small lake or a big pond. It was called Jacob's Lake. After unloading several hundred pounds' worth of building supplies, Sam and I had a good dinner of roast beef and potatoes. While we ate, Sam read his mail. Everywhere we stopped there had been messages or mail – his business was booming. That night we slept soundly.

The next morning, it was easy to see that we were no longer within sight of the Grand Canyon, and we hadn't seen it since we said farewell to Bill. I was disappointed. "Sam, how far are we from the Canyon?"

"I suppose it's thirty miles or so. Why?"

"I already miss it."

Sam chuckled. "We won't be close to the canyon again for several more days. Today we're headed to a little oasis in the middle of the desert called Pipe Spring. We'll spend the night there, and then we'll head back to St. George. That takes less than a day."

I was again disappointed. "When will we get back to the Canyon?"

"We'll probably turn around at St. George and head back to Pipe Spring. We did not bring all that Pipe Spring needed this trip, so we'll go right back there. It will be a heavy load, and we'll move slower. The rest of that next load of ours will all be more construction supplies for here at Jacob Lake, and some more supplies for Bill down at Bright Angel Point. Then we'll see."

As it turned out, Bill spent the summer going back and forth along that route, but when I got back to Bill's little Wylie Way Camp, I decided to stay there awhile. Bill was building cabins, and he said he could use my muscle. I obliged.

Sometimes, when he would go north to check on his concessions in Yellowstone, he left me in command and paid me extra. As I look back on those days, I think I worked there just to be next to the canyon.

+ + +

In late August of 1914, Bill was in camp working with me when Sam brought us a newspaper that was only a few days old. We learned that war had broken out in Europe, and that the United States was remaining neutral at that point in time. I was continuing to help with construction there on the rim, so I simply filed the information in the back of my mind. Bright Angel Point was becoming almost like home. Bill was paying me well, and I kept mailing checks into a savings account in St. George.

When the United States got into the war, many of our workers left to join the army. We had a minimal crew, many of them women, until early in the summer of 1919. One of the more attractive women flirted with me, but I was not ready for romance. When the war was over, tourists began to flock in. I said farewell to Bill and the rest of the crew, and I took a crude bus to St. George. Although I had been sending my income to my bank account there, I had no idea how much money I had saved. My needs were being met, so I had not had to trade for any gemstones in some time.

In St. George, I took a room at an old boarding house, and then I sat down with the manager of my bank. His name was Randy Thompson. "I've been mailing my endorsed paychecks to the bank for a long time." I handed him a slip of paper with my account number. "I want to see how much money I have in my account, and then I want to talk about investing at least some of it."

He nodded. "I'll check the ledgers. Please excuse me a moment." He left his desk, and he went behind the counter to some large books stacked on a table. He wrote on a slip of paper and came back to me. Sitting down, he smiled. "You've been depositing with us since 1912, and you've made no withdrawals. The total in your account right now, including interest, is $9,954.68. I heard you say that you want to invest some of this. There are several brokerage houses in St. George, and I recommend that you talk to John Spencer at Wells Fargo. Since this bank is not handling investments of stocks and bonds, but only real estate, I work with John, sending our customers to him. He sends real estate customers to me."

I nodded. "Thank you. I appreciate your advice. I will probably begin investing some of the money in my account later this week or the following week."

After standing and shaking his hand, I walked out of the bank and up the sidewalk. Wells Fargo was only two blocks up the street. After introducing myself, I sat down with John Spencer. "Since late in 1912, I've been working near the Grand Canyon, helping build a settlement. I've mailed my pay vouchers to the Bank of St. George. Earlier today, I met with Randy Thompson, and he recommended you to me. I want to make some stock investments. Right now, I just want information that

I can study. I'll be then praying about it before making my investments."

John nodded. "Prayer is always a good idea. There are no guarantees in the business of investments, but there are quite a few stock issues that are performing very well." He reached into a drawer of his desk, and he pulled out a large envelope. "I've prepared several envelopes like this for potential investors. There's information in here on a number of companies that may be of interest to you."

I was acutely aware that this was serious business, and I remained calm. "I will study this and pray about it. I plan on making some initial investments over the next two weeks."

The following Sunday, I went to Pine Valley Church, and I spent time in prayer both before and after the worship service. I did not have a lot of confidence in what I was about to do, but I knew that God had been watching over me, so I decided to take some risks. On Monday morning, I went to the Bank of St. George and sought out the manager. "Good morning, Randy. It's good to see you."

"Good morning, Mr. Tudor. What can I do for you today?"

"I've decided to proceed with making some investments. First, however, I would like to secure a safety deposit box, and I would like you to arrange a draft for five thousand dollars to Wells Fargo."

Randy nodded. "That will be fine. Is there anything else?"

"Yes. I would like to have you get me two thousand in gold pieces to put in my safety deposit box."

Again, Randy nodded. "Because of demand, we have enough 1920-S Double Eagles available. We can do all of this today."

"Good. I need my safe-deposit box to be sufficiently large for the coins, along with stock certificates and miscellaneous legal documents."

"Our largest box is currently five dollars per annum."

I nodded. That will be acceptable."

That night I examined my old trunk that I had brought from Scotland so many years earlier. First, I checked to be sure all the compartments I already knew about were empty. Three years before her death, Jacqueline had found a diamond hiding at the back of a drawer that I had long believed to be empty. I moved the trunk closer to the window, so I'd have plenty of light. It was like another mini-adventure!

During my search, I discovered that every drawer had a release tab, so I pulled all of them out. I shook them onto a linen pillowcase. As a result of that effort, several tiny gemstones appeared that had evidently gotten stuck in the linings of the drawers. Since I had several vials that I had purchased previously, I put thirty-seven tiny stones into one of the vials. None of them were more than a quarter carat.

As I started putting the drawers back in their slots, a glimmer inside caught my eye. Moments later, I took out a beautiful string of pearls. It was a string I had purchased for Sileas for our thirtieth anniversary. Evidently, our son, Arthur, had hidden the pearls there when he was hiding the gemstones.

Seeing it brought back beautiful memories, but there was no longer any pain. I set the string of pearls aside on a table and continued with my search.

As I put one of the larger drawers back in its slot, I spotted a tiny corner of a piece of paper protruding from a crevice. When I pulled on it, it tore off. I was curious about the crevice, so I slipped the blade of my pocket knife into where the piece of paper had been, and I worked it slowly along what appeared to be a crevice the entire depth of the trunk. The rest of the sheet of paper, whose corner I had torn off, came out with a sealed envelope. I recognized Jacqueline's handwriting.

> My dearest Brianan,
>
> As you may recall, when we first moved to Oakland, you secured cash for us by selling gemstones to Chao Lee in San Francisco. We had learned from several sources that he was a trustworthy jeweler. When you began making good money as a linguist, I put half of our surplus into our savings account. I took the other half to Chao Lee, and I bought gemstones. I thought they might be safer to have instead of money. If this displeases you, please forgive me.
>
> My love for you always, Jacqueline

When I opened the envelope, I was stunned. I got up, went to my upholstered chair, and sat down. My end table had a magnifying glass in the drawer, and I got it out. Then I had an idea. In my desk, I had a scale that measured weight in grams, and I knew there were five carats to a gram. In the envelope appeared to be a mixture of diamonds, rubies, sapphires, emeralds, and alexandrites. I sorted them into piles.

6 – diamonds about two to three carats each

2 – diamonds about five to six carats each

12 – rubies about five to eight carats each

9 – emeralds about five to six carats each

18 – sapphires about five to seven carats each

4 – alexandrites about three to five carats each

I put stones of each type into separate vials, and I scattered the vials among several drawers in the trunk. Sliding the trunk back into its usual place in the corner of my room, I went downstairs for dinner.

After my morning prayers and breakfast the next morning, I retrieved the vials from the trunk and put them in the inside pockets of my coat. Then I walked to the bank of St. George. I had an envelope containing stock certificates to put in my safety deposit box. With privacy, I also put the vials of gemstones in the box.

+ + +

For nearly ten years, I thrived in St. George. I continued to attend Pine Valley Church on Sundays, and each Monday morning I went over my records to see how my investments were doing. From time to time, I served as a translator for several businesses in the area. They paid well, and I invested most of the money as additions to my portfolio of stocks. Buying and selling stock was fun, and I was becoming wealthy. In 1924 I bought a house, paying cash for it, and moved out of the rooming house. Life was good. On the first Sunday of each month, I deposited a draft for ten percent of my earnings to Pine Valley Church. During the twenties, the church could do some long-needed repairs because of my donations. I agreed to be an elder in 1925.

On the first of September, 1926, John Spencer informed me that I was a millionaire. I was thrilled. I put on a barbeque in the back yard of my house, inviting more than fifty friends. I also hired some help to maintain my house and property. My portfolio of stocks began to grow even faster. Early in 1928, John told me that my portfolio was worth more than two million. I tried not to let it go to my head when so many women approached me with romance on their minds. Most of the approaches were sophisticated, but a few were not.

In October of 1929, the bubble burst. On "Black Tuesday," John Spencer told me about the stock market crash, giving me vivid details. Two days later, John committed suicide. On Friday, I went into the bank and talked with Randy. He told me that he planned to keep his employees, as long as he could. I took the stock certificates out of my box, and put them in envelopes. I took out a few of the gold pieces and put them in my pants pocket. When I got home, I dropped the envelopes into my steamer trunk as keepsakes, but I had little hope for the stocks' value long term.

Saturday, after John Spencer's funeral, I walked down to the Salvation Army shelter. The director, Paul Petersen, was a friend. "Hello, Paul, how are you doing?"

"Hello, Brianan, I'm blessed in the midst of all the difficulties. I hope you're here to make a donation." He smiled.

"What do you need the most?"

"Meat! When the crash struck, I had plenty of potatoes, carrots, and other veggies. I'm having a hard time getting meat, and I can't afford to buy it at this point."

I nodded. "I'll see what I can do. I'll check back later."

I walked out, turned right, and walked down to Big Al's meat market. Big Al came out to the counter when he heard me close the door. "Hi, Brianan. I hope you're planning another barbeque! I can use the business. Suddenly, no one can afford meat."

"Have you talked to Paul Petersen in the last few days?"

Al shook his head. "I haven't, but even if I had, I cannot afford to donate any meat. I've barely got enough business to stay afloat."

I looked at him straight in the eye. "If I give you a gold piece, how much beef can you deliver to Paul this afternoon?"

His eyes grew bigger. "Are you serious?"

I nodded. "Yep."

"How about a hundred pounds?"

"Can you make it a hundred and a quarter?"

He gave me a pained look. "Okay, Brianan, but you're really cutting into my profit."

"Thank you, Al." I handed him a gold piece.

"Thank you! I'll get right on it."

I headed home. In front, Hank Shuffett was watering my flower beds. He and his wife, Hazel, had been working for me for over three years. She was a terrific cook, and she did a credible job keeping things clean and in order inside. They lived less than a mile away in town. "Good afternoon, Hank."

"Good afternoon, sir. Hazel and I have been wondering if we're going to lose our jobs."

I shook my head. "No, Hank, I plan on keeping you both here for the foreseeable future. In fact, if you and Hazel want to move your stuff out of that flat you have been living in downtown, you can move into the spare bedroom in back here, if you wish."

His eyes got wide. "That would be great! The rent money can go for other things. Let me run inside and tell Hazel." He turned off the water and went inside.

I went in a moment later, and Hazel approached. "Thank you, Brianan!" She gave me a hug. "You know we'll earn our keep!

9.
Academic Life

Life in St. George became a struggle for everyone I knew. I had lost more than two million dollars when the stock market crashed, but I had my house, some twenty-dollar gold pieces, and the gemstones. Judging from stories in the newspaper, it was the same everywhere. I put a gold piece in the offering at Pine Valley Church every Sunday.

From time to time, I would mail a few gemstones to Chao Lee in San Francisco, and he would send cash back to me in the mail within a week. I did not know how old Mr. Lee was, but he was not young. He did have seven sons, five daughters, and numerous grandchildren. I knew that I could depend on him still.

On Christmas Eve, 1934, I went to the late-night worship service at Pine Valley Church. I thought it started at 10:30, but I found out when I got there that it did not start until 11:00. I went in and sat down to pray. As I prayed, I became aware of someone sitting beside me, but I continued to pray.

"Brianan, I have not appeared to you since before Jacqueline died. There will be others arriving in less than ten minutes, so listen."

I opened my eyes and saw the same angel that I had seen previously. "It was hard losing Jacqueline, you know."

"I know, but she is safe and secure with our Creator. Another change will happen in your life this coming summer. There will be people from Texas wanting to talk with you. They will question your ability with languages. They've heard stories from San Francisco about that gift the Lord God gave you, and they find it difficult to believe. If they offer you a job, you need to go. Just leave the house with Hazel and Hank, and go where the people from Texas tell you. Your country will go to war again soon, but you must stay in Fort Worth."

As I gazed at her, she vanished, and a moment later, pastor Bob came in the door. I closed my eyes and continued to pray until the worship service started.

In July of 1935, I got a letter from Texas Christian University in Fort Worth.

> Dear Mr. Tudor,
>
> For the past six years, members of our faculty who teach Mandarin Chinese and other languages have been hearing stories about you and your translational abilities. People utilizing your services have said that you can learn to speak a language in less than a day. Personally, I find this difficult to believe, so I would like to talk with you. Others would like to talk with you as well.
>
> Please respond at your earliest convenience. If possible, we would like you to travel by train here to Fort Worth.
>
> Sincerely,
>
> Samuel L. Greely

I sent him a telegram in response, and I spent the last week of July and the first week of August going to and from Fort Worth.

As it turned out, the School of Liberal Arts had prepared some challenges for me. The Mayor of Fort Worth, Van Zandt Jarvis, along with his wife, took me to dinner along with another man, who ostensibly did not speak English. As we ate, I tried communicating with the man, pointing at various items on our table and saying the English word for that item, and then pointing at him. He quickly got the idea and spoke his word for that item. Next, I put the English words in sentences, and after that pointing again at him. When it was time to order dessert, I could explain his choices in his language. As we ate dessert, I continued to converse with him.

When the waiter brought brandy, the man spoke with the mayor in perfect English. "Dr. Jarvis, I must tell you that I am truly amazed. In a little over an hour, Mr. Tudor here has acquired a working knowledge of my native tongue, Siamese. He seems to have a rare gift."

The mayor's mouth hung open for a moment, then he closed it. "You're serious, aren't you?"

"Yes, sir. I understand that you have arranged for another challenge for him for tomorrow at lunch. May I join the three of you, just to listen?"

Van Jarvis nodded. "That can be arranged." He turned to me. "Tell me, Mr. Tudor, when did you first start doing this?"

As I responded, I did not mention Jacqueline so that the time frame would be more believable. "I was traveling from Pierre, South Dakota to Yellowstone. I encountered some Shoshones, who were hunting and curious about me, and they wanted to know who I was. As I listened to them talk with each other and then attempt to talk with me, I discovered my gift. In about an hour, I was chatting with them. We traveled together for two days."

"I'm told that you don't know any written languages other than English, is that correct?"

I shook my head. "No. My late wife's native tongue was French, and she taught me to write some French as well as speak it. When I came from Wales, I could read, write, and speak in English, Welsh, Scots, and Irish."

"How many languages do you speak?"

I was thoughtful. "I have a speaking knowledge of English, Scots, Welsh, Gaelic, Irish, Mandarin Chinese, French, Spanish, and German. I do fairly well in half-dozen others, and then I've dabbled briefly with about a dozen others like my latest, Siamese, and some American Indian dialects. I would have to spend at least a week, preferably a month, talking with this man before I would feel as though I was reasonably fluent enough in his language to teach it. It would take a little longer to gain a written knowledge."

At dinner that evening, I found both Mr. & Mrs. Jarvis and Mr. Arthit Bhuvanath (the other man) to be very interesting people. Arthit was on the TCU faculty at the time, and Mr. Jarvis was part of the administration.

Lunch the next day presented a greater challenge to my skills. Before lunch, Van, Arthit, and an unnamed woman walked about on the TCU campus with me for a half hour. I tried my best to converse a little with her before going to lunch. I was feeling mostly lost, picking up only a couple of useful words and phrases.

When we started eating, coffee was brought to us. She thanked the waiter for the coffee, and a lingual connection was suddenly made in my mind all at once. Everything else she had said made sense, and I began conversing with her rather easily. She smiled as we began to converse freely, and Van and Arthit were then totally lost.

Arthit looked at me. "What language is she speaking?"

I shook my head, looked at her, and asked her in her tongue.

In perfect English, she responded, "The language I've been speaking is a dialect of Hindi from northern India." She turned to me. "For the rest of our meal, let's talk in English for the sake of Arthit and Van." The rest of lunch was very enjoyable.

The following day, I got on a train for my return trip to St. George. I was not offered a job at TCU, but because of what the angel had told me, I knew that eventually they would do so. I had plenty of time to plan my departure from St. George, from Utah, and from another phase of my life.

I wrote to my son in Oakland.

> Dear James,
>
> In light of the secret I've shared with you, I trust your judgment as to whether or not you share this letter with your siblings, and if you do, how much of it you share is also up to you.
>
> The work in Las Vegas did not work out, and I began to explore Zion Canyon, Bryce Canyon, and the Grand Canyon. I ended up helping build a settlement on the North Rim of the Grand Canyon at a place called Bright Angel Point. It is amazingly beautiful there. Lately I've been living in St. George, Utah, but that is about to change.
>
> I'm going to move to Fort Worth, Texas soon. Please know that you and the rest of the family are in my prayers. I love you.

I mailed the letter within a week after I returned to St. George. For two more Sundays, I put a gold piece in the offering. I got a letter from Samuel Greely thanking me for coming to Fort Worth. He said he was sorry we had not met, but he was in Houston with family while I was in Fort Worth.

That following weekend, I asked Randy from the Bank of St. George to meet me at Big Al's Meat Market. Previously, I had sold two of my larger gemstones and had deposited the money in my checking account. At the meat market, Randy was a witness as Big Al agreed to supply meat to the Salvation Army Shelter, for which I agreed to have the bank send a draft each week. At the bank, I signed a recurring draft order with Randy.

The next day, I got a letter from Van Jarvis.

> Dear Brianan,

I'm writing to offer you a pair of jobs. Speaking as the Mayor, The City of Fort Worth would like to put you on part-time salary as our translator-on-call.

As an administrator at Texas Christian University, I'm offering you your second job, as Adjunct Professor of Languages. Samuel Greely will have class assignments for you, if you accept, after you arrive. Please let me know as soon as possible if you accept the offers of these two jobs.

I sent telegrams of acceptance to both Van Jarvis and Sam Greely.

That evening, after dinner, I sat down with Hank and Hazel. "I have some important things to tell you both. First, I have been offered work in Fort Worth, Texas, and I'll be leaving in three days. I'll need both of you to help me pack and take my effects to the train station."

Hazel's eyes grew big. "How long will you be there?"

I smiled. "For all intents and purposes, this is a permanent move, Hazel, so that's why I must make arrangements with you two. Since I am leaving the house and the land to you, I have some suggestions for you."

Hank's mouth hung open. "Did you say that you're leaving the house and the land to us?"

I nodded and smiled. "Yes, I am. The two of you have been invaluable to me. You have been a great help as I have helped others in St. George deal with these hard times. I suggest that you turn this house into a rooming house. As you know, three of the bedrooms in this house have gone unused since I moved in. There's also an attic as well as a basement."

Hazel was thoughtful. "I have such mixed feelings. We'll miss you terribly, of course, and this seems so sudden!"

I nodded. "I know." I reached inside my pants pocket and took out ten gold pieces. I put them on the table. "The deed will be put in both your names tomorrow morning. This is a hundred dollars. You can use it to make the attic livable, to clean and furnish the unused bedrooms, and to stock the basement for yourselves and your tenants. Maybe you can offer a month of free room and board in exchange for labor to do the modifications to the house."

Hank shook my hand. "We can never thank you enough, Brianan."

I nodded. "Let's keep one another in our prayers, shall we?"

They agreed.

+ + +

Before I took the train to Fort Worth, Randy used his connections and helped me set up a checking account with Fort Worth National Bank. I wrote to Chao Lee, and in my letter, which was sent by a private messenger service, I enclosed some larger gemstones along with my Fort Worth National Bank checking account number.

A few days later, I received a receipt from Chao Lee. He told me that his son, Duke, would soon be taking over the business. I suspected, when I read that receipt, that I would undoubtedly find a few more gemstones in the old trunk, and I would be continuing to business with Chao and Duke for the foreseeable future.

When I arrived in Fort Worth, I went house hunting. Just north of the university on Princeton Avenue, I purchased a three-bedroom house from a bank that had foreclosed on its mortgage. By the time the first semester of classes started, I had my house fully furnished, and I had food in my pantry and in my icebox.

Sam Greely started me with a light class load. "I don't want you to be overwhelmed by your first semester or two of university life on campus. You're teaching classes in Welsh and Gaelic, which are firsts for TCU, and you're working in the library to help foreign students who struggle with English."

I nodded. "I want to start working on a Bachelor's degree for myself as well."

Sam raised his eyebrows. "Really? I'll arrange for you to have a discount on tuition because you're on staff. What do you want to study?"

"I don't know where my focus will be, so I'll start by taking basic courses in history, math, and science. I'll choose a focus later." After showing me my classrooms and office, Sam took me to register with other students.

My first Sunday in town, I attended a worship service at University Christian Church, which was across the street from the university. I liked the people, and I put a gold piece in the offering plate. After church, I talked with several people. I was approached by a distinguished-looking man. "Good morning! I'm George Armstrong."

I smiled and nodded. "I'm Brianan Tudor. Are you a member of this congregation?"

He nodded. "Yes. I'm the head of Texas Steel. My wife, Catherine, is around here somewhere."

I nodded. "I'm not married. I recently joined the staff of TCU as a language teacher and linguist, and I'm on call to the Mayor's Office as a translator."

He smiled. "That's very interesting! What languages are you teaching, Spanish, French, or German?"

I shook my head. "I'm not teaching those languages this semester. For the first time in the university's history, I'm teaching Welsh and Gaelic. I don't think those two languages are being taught anywhere else in Texas."

He stared at me. "How many languages do you speak?"

"I speak nine fluently, and of those nine I read and write in five with good grammar. With fair fluency, I can speak in a half-dozen more, and I communicate somewhat in another dozen. It's a God-given gift."

He nodded. "That is indeed a God-given gift. How is it that you can teach Welsh and Gaelic?"

I smiled. "I was born in Ireland, and as a child moved to Scotland. Then I moved to Wales, and later came to the United States."

"Are you renting space here?"

I shook my head. "I purchased a house up the street on Princeton Avenue. Do you live here in Fort Worth?"

He shook his head. "My wife and I live in Dallas, but she's from Fort Worth, so we come here almost every weekend."

That was a conversation that led to a lasting friendship. Gradually, I made my way through the after-church crowd and walked home. As I walked up the steps and onto my porch, I heard a voice behind me.

"Excuse me!"

I turned and saw a young man in his late teens. "Yes, can I help you?"

He walked up and offered his hand. "I'm Dan Holton. I'm a TCU sophomore. My first year I lived in a dorm, but I'm wanting to get away from dorm life. I know this house used to be for sale, so evidently you have bought it. By any chance, do you have a room for rent?"

I shook my head. "I've not considered it. I've just accepted a position as an adjunct professor. Why don't you come in? We'll have some lemonade, and we'll talk about it?"

He seemed like a nice guy, but I decided that being a landlord was not for me. He was a musician, and I knew that I would not want him practicing in the house or bringing over other musicians.

When classes started, my most interesting hours were spent with my first-year Welsh students. There were seventeen of them. The first week, I taught them the history of Scotland, speaking to them in Welsh as much as possible, and inviting them to respond as best they could. On Friday of that first week, I talked about romance in the British Isles, and the students began flirting with one another. The boys were fairly clumsy, but the girls quickly caught on to the ways of Welsh culture.

My first-year Gaelic class was not as much fun for me because it was larger, and I focused upon teaching them some basic vocabulary and grammar. Still, I realized that God had given me some good basic teaching skills. I taught on Mondays, Wednesdays, and Fridays, and on Tuesdays and Thursdays, I attended my own classes in history, math, and science. At times, I felt overwhelmed, but I loved it.

On my second Tuesday of the semester, I went into the cafeteria to have a hot lunch. I took my tray to a small empty table and sat down. Just as I began to eat, a woman approached me.

"Excuse me, my name is Debra Chabert. I teach in the school of nursing. Aren't you on the faculty as well?"

I stood up to greet her and nodded. "Yes, I teach languages. My name is Brianan Tudor. Would you like to join me?"

She nodded. "Thank you." She sat down. "Brianan, you did not say you taught a particular language, but instead you simply said you teach languages. Why is that?"

I swallowed some coffee and smiled. "This is my first semester, and I'm teaching Welsh and Gaelic, probably the only such classes within the state. I don't know what I will be teaching next semester, let alone next year. You said you teach nursing. Are you a registered nurse?"

She nodded. "Yes. I'm head of the nursing staff at Harris Methodist Hospital. Two days each week I teach advanced nursing classes here at TCU."

As she spoke, I studied her face. Why did God constantly put stunningly beautiful redheads in my path? Dearbhail, Sileas, and Jacqueline had all been redheads. This one had lots of beautiful freckles. "I decided you were a nurse, Debra, because that pin on your lapel is a Caduceus."

She smiled. "You're a knowledgeable man, Brianan. How many languages do you speak?"

I told her how I had answered that question from George Armstrong. Then I said, "I may have reasons to use my knowledge of American Indian dialects here in Texas."

She nodded. "That's an amazing gift. Yes, there's a variety of tribes represented in the Lone Star State. Last year, I cared for a patient from the Kickapoo Tribe and learned a few words of his language."

I nodded. "That's one of the Fox family of languages. I discovered my gift when I encountered some Shoshones in Montana." We finished our lunch. "Would you like to join me for dinner this evening? I'm told that there's great food at the Arlington Steak House."

She smiled. "I'd love to!"

From the beginning, when I picked Debra up for dinner that evening, I felt warm, and my heart beat faster. That had not happened before. I married Dearbhail less than a month after I met her simply because it seemed like I should. As naturally quiet as Dearbhail was, we gradually fell in love. With Sileas, we fell in love as we courted. With Jacqueline, we emotionally bonded after a few weeks, but there was no romance until we said our vows. In many ways, Debra was different from all three of them.

Debra and I went to church every Sunday. I introduced her to George and Catherine Armstrong. After worshiping together for the first time, over lunch she revealed something that was incredibly important to both of us. "Brianan, I try to make a conscious effort to be like Jesus. Does that sound strange to you?"

I looked straight into her eyes, knowing that I was already helplessly in love with her. "It not only isn't strange, it is important to me. Some of my earliest recollections of childhood in Scotland involve talking with Jesus as a family."

Debra smiled, reached across our table, and put her hand on top of mine. "God bless us!"

"Amen."

We fell in love with one another very quickly. On December 20, 1935, Debra and I were married in the university's chapel. For our honeymoon, I took her to Carlsbad Caverns because of her interest in seeing them.

Both of us wanted to have a family, but it was not to be. We had three pregnancies in just over three years, but all of them miscarried. For Debra, it was devastating, but she tried not to show it. We kept trying. As war began to ferment in Europe, many of Debra's students wanted to talk about battlefield nursing. It took Debra's mind off of her emotional pain, at least part of the time.

On December 7, 1941, our world suddenly changed. When the Japanese attacked Pearl Harbor, it was a shock to the entire country. Many of the students at TCU decided to suspend their studies and join in the fighting. At church, George and Catherine talked about him enlisting, but his company was going to supply much of the steel for the war effort. Most of Debra's students wanted to talk about what extra preparations they could make before volunteering to serve in the military.

The Friday of that first week after the attack, one of my students, Barry London, approached me. "Mr. Tudor, do you know anything about the Choctaw Code Talkers of the First World War?"

I nodded. "I was not involved, but I have a few Choctaw friends. Why do you ask, Barry?"

He looked around, and then spoke quietly. "My Dad has a friend named Philip Johnston. Our government is considering using Comanche code talkers in Europe, but Mr. Johnston is pressing for the use of Navajo code talkers in the Pacific war."

I thought carefully. "That makes sense. Navajo is still not a written language, and it has very complex grammar. Of all the American Indian languages, it could prove to be the most useful. Why are you asking?"

"I told my dad that you were fluent in American Indian languages, and he wants you to talk with Philip Johnston."

"Thanks, Barry. I'll pray about it and let you know."

10.
Into World War II

That evening, Debra and I were relaxing after dinner. She drew close to me. "Brianan, so many of my friends are going to London to do what they can. When we worship and pray together later, we need to talk to the Lord about whether or not I should go."

I put my arm around her. "Okay. I have a prayer request too. Do you remember ever reading about how during the First World War, the Choctaw Indians used their native language to be code talkers?"

"I remember. My mother had a friend who was half Choctaw, and she was involved in that effort."

"I was approached by a student today. His Dad has a friend named Philip Johnson, who is pressing for the use of Navajo code talkers against the Japanese. I told him that it made sense for two reasons. There's no written Navajo language, and the grammar of their language is complex. We need to pray about whether I should talk to Philip Johnston and get involved with code talking."

When Debra and I prayed together, we always prayed aloud and talked to the Lord informally. It would have shocked Dearbhail, because she insisted that I do all the praying and expected me to be very Biblical and formal. With Sileas, she joined me in prayer, but we both prayed formally. Prayers with Jacqueline had evolved over the decades we were together. Debra and I also listened for the Lord's silent voice moving our thoughts. When that happened to either of us, Debra or I would respond aloud immediately to what the Lord seemed to be saying. As a result, it often seemed like a three-way conversation, where only the Lord's voice could not be heard audibly.

That night, we both ended up knowing that Debra would eventually go to London, and I was going to start working with the Navajos after talking with Philip Johnston. After making love, we slept soundly.

Both of us continued with our work at TCU as we watched expectantly to see what developed. Philip Johnston and I found that we had many thoughts in common, and telegrams began going back and forth between us. I sent him some detailed suggestions throughout the code talker project, but I did so by letter for security reasons. Most of my Navajo friends lived in Arizona and Utah. I utilized my contacts in Lee's Ferry and St. George. Progress was slow.

Meanwhile, Debra frequently talked with the wife of the former governor of Texas, William Hobby. Her name was Oveta. Over lunch one day, Oveta was livid. "In May of last year, Congresswoman Rogers introduced a bill to establish a Women's Army Auxiliary Corps. It stalled until General Marshall got involved, but even with his support, along with the support of Eleanor Roosevelt, it was virtually dead. Then General Marshall, bless his soul, ordered the War Department to create the Corps. Army nurses were at Pearl Harbor on December 7, 1941, yet again the Bill introduced by Congresswoman Rogers was amended and stalled to death. I'd like to go to Washington and shoot some of those blockheads!"

Debra smiled. "We've known each other for five years, Oveta. This isn't the first time that you and other women's groups have been stonewalled. It's been going on here in Texas all of my life!"

A waiter approached and handed Mrs. Hobby a telegram. Oveta's eyes flashed back and forth. "Well, it's about time! The Bill passed!" She looked at Debra. Now, maybe we can get a truly effective nurse corps established.

Debra nodded. "Let's hope so. I wonder who will head it up?"

The answer came that evening, when President Roosevelt signed the bill into law. He appointed Oveta the first director of the Women's Army Auxiliary Corps. Ten days later, Oveta and Debra had lunch together again.

Oveta looked at Debra. "Where do you want to serve, dear? As director, I can arrange for you to go wherever you think you're needed."

My wife swallowed. "I've thought about it, and I've prayed about it, Oveta. I don't have my husband's gift for languages, so I think it's best if I go to London."

Meanwhile, Debra and I were still trying to start a family. Just before she left in June of 1942, we thought maybe she had gotten pregnant. A rabbit test proved us wrong. The night before she took a train to New York, we made love and cried together.

+ + +

With Debra in London, I focused upon work, both on and off campus. There was increasing demand for learning the languages of Europe, particularly German. I took on a nearly double class load.

On the Fourth of July, 1942, Sam Greely called me. "Hi, Brianan. Are you having a fun Fourth?"

"Not with Debra in London, I'm not, Sam. How are you doing?"

"Oh, we're not spending money on fireworks. Brooke and I are having a quiet Fourth at home. Besides wishing you a happy Fourth of July, Brianan, I'm calling on a University matter. Can you speak Japanese?"

I hesitated. "Yes, I can, Sam, but I'm pretty rusty. Why, does TCU want me to teach a Japanese class in September?"

"Yes, Brianan, but before you do, we've arranged for you to visit one of the Japanese internment camps, the one in Rohwer, Arkansas."

I was silent.

"Brianan? Are you still there?"

"I'm here." I paused. "Those internment camps are wrong, Sam, and you and I both know it. It is going to be a dark page in our country's history."

"I know, Brianan, but that's not the point right now."

"Right, it's all in the name of the war effort. Okay, I'll go, but I still will have to have the last two weeks of August and the first week of September for the Navajo Code Talkers project. Make sure that is cleared on my calendar for the university."

"Okay, Brianan. I don't think you'll be sorry that you agreed to do these things."

"We'll see, Sam."

After hanging up, I dialed zero. "Operator, please connect me with the offices of the Red Cross in Texarkana."

Yes, sir."

"Thank you."

More than a minute passed silently by. "Red Cross of Texarkana. How may I help you?"

"Yes, I'm inquiring into the conditions of the Japanese internment camp in Rohwer, Arkansas. Are those who are interred there having all their needs met?"

"Who is this?"

"This is Brianan Tudor, professor of languages at Texas Christian University."

"Well, Mr. Tudor, I'm not authorized to be very specific, but I can at least truthfully say that conditions there are humane."

"That's not what I'm asking. TCU is sending me there to talk with some of the Japanese Americans interned there in order to brush up on my language skills. Unfortunately, it's my job to do this. If I arrange for a donation to your office of the Red Cross, can you assure me that the donation will be entirely used to help those interred there in Rohwer? I do not want credit for the donation, but I want to be sure that it is helpful to those people."

"I give you my word, sir. I will see to it as best I can. When will you be there?"

"I'm supposed to arrive there in a few days. Again, sir, I do not want attention drawn to myself."

"Very well, sir."

I hung up.

The university arranged for about two dozen Japanese Americans to meet with me at the camp. They were supposed to be people who mostly accepted their situation and would be willing to help. Getting there by a combination of train and car, it took the better part of a day. After spending the night in a barrack set aside for camp support personnel, and after breakfast the next morning, I was led to a large meeting hall.

As I requested, chairs had been arranged in a circle, and I sat down in one of them. "Good morning." There were murmurs of good morning from around the room. "I have mixed feelings about being here, and I will explain why if you wish me to. This is not about my feelings, however." I paused and took a deep breath.

"My name is Brianan Tudor. I'm a Scottish American, and I am on the faculty of Texas Christian University in Fort Worth. I have a peculiar gift. It is a gift of learning languages quickly. Aside from English, I speak, read, and write five European languages, I speak several fluently. I am moderately conversant in a few more, and I can marginally communicate in a dozen more." I saw a hand go up, but I smiled and said, "One moment more, please."

"Because of an event in St. George, Utah, a few years ago, Japanese was one of those languages in which I am moderately conversant. Currently, I am assisting our government and a number of Navajo Indians in creating a code-talk system, similar to the one used by the Choctaw Code Talkers in the first World War. The Navajo system we are developing should be far more effective for two reasons. There is no Navajo written language, and their grammar is extremely complicated. I am not expecting any of you to be able to speak Navajo."

There were smiles around the circle. The woman who had raised her hand raised it again. She spoke flawless English. "Are you wanting us to help you improve your Japanese?"

I nodded. "I need to be able to teach spoken Japanese effectively next month. I will be here a week, or perhaps a little longer if necessary." They looked around at one another, and then they nodded to one another.

For the next nine days, I was with them day and night. I do not know how good the food there was, either before or after I was there, but it was excellent during those nine days. One of the first things I told them, in Japanese, was that I believed that their interment was both unjust and unfair. There were a few Christians among them, and I prayed with them each day.

On the Sunday I was there, I went into the camp chapel with some of them. A few who were not Christians went with us, praise God. Some of them were quite angry with our government. Most of them had the wisdom to know that during the war was not the time to fight their situation or create problems.

While dinner was being served one evening, I saw a vaguely familiar face. It took me a moment, but then I recognized him. He came to my table to serve, and I greeted him. "Good evening, Dan, I barely recognized you." I turned towards the rest of the people at my table. "Ladies and gentleman, this is Dan Holton. When I last saw him, he was an undergraduate music student at TCU." I turned back to him. "Are you a graduate student now?"

He nodded. "Yes, Mr. Tudor." He smiled. "You remembered that I'm a musician. No, I'm not a graduate student. I am putting on performances with a small band in an entertainment troupe with the USO. Here at Rohwer, however, I'm simply volunteering. My fiancée teaches advanced cooking classes in high schools in Fort Worth. She decided to do some volunteer teaching here at Rohwer. She's been here since the first of August. If I may ask your friends here, has the food been any better here during the last couple of weeks?"

All of them smiled and nodded. Hank, one of my most helpful friends, said, "It seems that Mr. Tudor's presence here this month has had an unintended positive effect!" The rest of them nodded.

Dan went back to serve. By the time I left, all of them knew how to reach me after the war at TCU. As left, I knew that I had made some friends. I was glad that I went.

Sam Greely met me at the train station in Fort Worth. "Brianan! It's good to see you! Did you achieve what you wanted to? Are you glad you went?"

I nodded. "The answer is yes to both of your questions. The camps are unjust and unfair, but it is war. That's a poor and inadequate excuse, but it is the only excuse our government has."

"Are you ready to teach Japanese?" We got into his car.

"I'm definitely ready. They even gave me a working knowledge of their alphabet."

"Excellent! I've been getting messages regarding the Code Talkers project almost every day. The day-after tomorrow, you're coming back to this station, and you are going to El Paso." He pulled the car out of the parking lot. "You and the others will be staying at the Hotel Cortez and having your meetings there. What, may I ask, is your part in all of this?"

I knew this question was coming, both right then and in El Paso. "I have two advantages that the others do not. First, I speak Navajo fluently out of personal experience, but I am an outsider, and as an outsider, I can see things that they can do with their language that perhaps they cannot see. The second reason is my fluency with other languages enables me to see tricks that the Navajos can do with their own language to create a code. Even most Navajos listening to these talking the code might not be able to decipher what they say. I've been working with them by mail."

That first day in the Hotel Cortez was the only time I met and talked with Philip Johnson in person. He did a great job of getting Washington to approve and fund the project, but he was a civil engineer, and he knew nothing about languages. He went home after dinner the first day.

The code talk was, to a large extent, already worked out at Camp Pendleton in California the previous spring. The purpose of this meeting was to fine-tune the code and develop special codes for special situations. All of them were U.S. Marines, and they were tough. Some tactics and concepts, as well as tools of warfare, were given uniquely Navajo terms. A "shark" was a navy destroyer; "go-fasters" were running shoes; and the Navajo term for a pen was "ink-stick." It was brilliantly simple in a rather obtuse way. You had to know the special Navajo terms in use in order to understand the code, even if you were a Navajo. The government was printing out their code book in English even as we met. They were designed as loose-leaf, so that specific areas could be easily updated as situations dictated.

Although the Marines recruited about two hundred to be code-talkers, I was told that I was one of only nineteen people around the world – as far as they knew – who were not native speakers of Navajo. I was complimented several times that week on my abilities with their language.

+ + +

When I got back to my house in Fort Worth, there was a telegram in my mailbox.

> Dear Mr. Tudor,
>
> We regret to inform you that your wife, Debra, has been killed in an automobile accident forty-seven miles east of London. As you know, she was the staff charge nurse for the military chiefs of staff in the bunker below the city.
>
> General Dwight Eisenhower has posted a personal and detailed letter to you expressing his deep regrets, and you will probably be receiving that letter within two to three weeks. She was a brilliant and amazingly capable woman.
>
> George Patton

I sat on a chair for hours, staring into space. What happens now? Is this part of God's plan? When the sun went down, for a while I stared into the darkness. The phone rang, and I picked it up. "Hello?"

"Hi, Brianan, this is Sam. When did you get in?" I didn't answer at first. "Brianan, are you there?"

"Yes, Sam, I'm here. Debra was killed in an automobile accident three days ago. I learned it from a telegram."

"I'll be right over." He hung up.

I continued to sit in the dark, staring into space. I don't know how long it was before I heard a knock on the door. "Come in." The door opened. The lights came on, and several people came in.

"We're so sorry, Brianan." Sam was shaking his head.

I nodded. "Thank you." I stood up and looked around. The room seemed impossibly full of people. I looked around. "Thank you, everyone." I paused. "So, that everyone knows the facts, and nobody has to do guesswork, here's all I know. Getting back to my house, there was a telegram. Debra was killed in an automobile accident, on a road just east of London. It happened three days ago. She was probably buried with full military honors. She was the nurse in residence for the Chiefs of Staff of the Allied Forces. General Eisenhower has dictated a letter I should get in a few days. That's all I know right now." I sat down again, and everyone talked quietly. Food came from somewhere, and I ate, though I did not enjoy it.

I do not know how many people finally came. A number of Debra's students and former students were there. Other teachers and staff, Van Jarvis, the campus pastor, and still others came and went. In the early evening, George and Catherine Armstrong came, and they sat with me for a while.

The next day, I called Sam Greely. "Sam, I cannot just sit here, so when this semester's registrations begin on Monday, I'll be there. I've only two semesters left before I'll receive my Bachelor of Education. Is my teaching schedule on my desk?"

"Yes, Brianan, but if you need to take time off...."

"No." I interrupted him. "I have to work. My schedule?"

"You're teaching three classes of Japanese, with class sizes limited to twenty-five each. You're also teaching one each of Scots, Welsh, Gaelic, and advanced German. That's the heaviest load you've ever had, but you'll be paid well for it."

I threw myself into getting registered for the three classes that I needed, and then I began preparing to work. For a couple of weeks, I cried myself to sleep at night, but gradually that subsided. With the heavy class load, in all but the Japanese classes, I graded papers into the night, or worked on my own homework, often past midnight. At least I was exhausted enough to sleep when I turned off the light.

In my mailbox, the next morning there was a letter with an Arkansas postmark.

> Dear Mr. Tudor,
>
> You probably do not remember me. I am the chaplain in the Japanese internment camp in Rohwer, Arkansas. That Sunday morning you worshiped with us, you brought several Japanese with you, some of whom were not Christians. The following week, there were still more. In the weeks since, I have had the privilege of baptizing eleven Japanese who have given their lives to Jesus. I don't know what you talked about with them that week, but you evidently had a profound influence. God bless you!
>
> Roland Massey, Chaplain

I smiled, looked up, and closed my eyes. "Thank you, Lord!"

Two weeks later, a U.S. Army lieutenant knocked on my door in the evening. As I opened the door, he spoke. "Mr. Tudor?"

"Yes."

"My name is Bill Trump. I'm a lieutenant stationed at Love Field in Dallas." He handed me an envelope. "I'm home on emergency leave. I've come from London, England, and General Eisenhower asked me to deliver this personally to you."

"Thank you, lieutenant. Would you like to come in and have some coffee?"

"Thank you, no, sir, my wife is waiting for me." He turned crisply, and he walked off my porch.

I opened the envelope as I walked inside. It was surprisingly long, and it was not at all formal. I still have the letter among my papers that I've kept in my old trunk.

It was a busy semester, and that was good. Immersing myself in my work, I could set aside my pain. Debra had filled my life with incredible joy.

On the day after Thanksgiving, my phone rang. "Hello?"

Hi, Brianan, this is Dibe Smith. We worked together in El Paso for the Code Talkers project."

"Hello, Dibe, what's up?"

"I was so sorry to hear about Debra. How are you doing?"

I responded in Navajo, "I'm making work my passion, and my grief, as God heals me. She loves God in person now."

He grunted. "Yes." He also spoke Navaho. "I'm taking two weeks for leave from the Marines for Christmas and New Years. I'm going skiing in Taos. Do you want to join me?"

"What about your fiancé, Susan?"

"She married a farmer while I was stationed in Hawaii."

"I'm sorry."

"It's just as well. What about skiing with me?"

"I should probably get away from here for a few days, Dibe. Okay, it will be good. When shall I meet you and where?"

I've got reservations at Taos Inn from December 21st to January 2nd. See you there."

"Okay, see you then, Dibe."

+ + +

The Taos Inn was offering servicemen rates that were 80% off. I decided that, with my recently increased salary as a full professor, I could afford things better than he could. I convinced Dibe to let me pay for the hotel, and we agreed to split the costs of food and drink. The food was outstanding, and the hotel was very comfortable and rather new.

At first, Dibe and I tried snow-shoeing, and then we tried cross-country skiing. We later took ski instruction classes. Even though Dibe was visibly younger because of streaks of gray in my hair, I took to the skiing more easily. I had not skied since I left Scotland, but it quickly came back to me.

There was a ski lift powered by an old steam engine, and Dibe and I decided we wanted some higher scenery. When we got near the top, Dibe was impressed. "Wow! I've faced some scary stuff before, but this is kind of different."

I was thrilled, and I grinned. "This looks like fun! Sometimes we just have to learn things by doing it. The easy trail down is off to our right, and the intermediate and difficult trails are this way." I pointed. "What do you want to try?"

Dibe grinned. "Please don't think me chicken, but I want to be able to go back to my platoon in one piece. This is my first time downhill, so let's start with the easy trail."

I shrugged. "Okay." I started down, and I heard him starting to follow behind me. It was kind of fun, but I knew I had to take a greater risk. At the bottom, when we met near the lift, looked at him. "That was okay, Dibe, but this next time I want to try that intermediate trail through the trees."

He nodded. "Okay. I'm game."

At the top, I looked at him. "Do you want to go first this time, or do you want to follow me?"

He started down the hill. I waited about ten seconds, and then I followed him. It was exhilarating. As the trees flew by, my heart beat faster. I felt better than I had in weeks – since I had lost Debra.

At the bottom, Dibe was grinning. "That was great! Let's do that one again!"

I agreed. We took intermediate trails on through the next several days. Late in the afternoon on New Years Eve, I told Dibe that I wanted to try one of the advanced trails. He shook his head. "No thanks, I don't have the skills. You're better at this than I am."

"I'll go down with you." It was the ski instructor, Johnny. "My wife sold you your lift tickets. You're Brianan Tudor, aren't you?" I nodded. "I've watched you. You can do that northwest trail. I can lead you down."

I shrugged. "Okay." Dibe went with us up to the top, but when Dibe started down one of the intermediate trails, we waited.

"Are you ready," Johnny asked.

I nodded, and we were off. I doubt that I ever skied even close to that fast in Scotland. A couple of times, I was truly scared, but I loved it! Johnny and I had been at the ski shelter a minute or two when Dibe joined us. "You guys are nuts! I watched you. That was crazy fast!"

I grinned. "I was pretty scared a couple of times, but I'm glad I did it."

The next morning, Dibe had to catch a bus west to Albuquerque, so that he could get a military transport that flew from there back to San Diego. We said our farewells, and I took a different bus, going north to Durango. There I got on a train that took me into Fort Worth.

11.
Becoming a Pastor

When I was sleeping in a Pullman Car going back to Fort Worth from Durango, it seemed as though Debra spoke to me when I was doing Bible study and praying. It seemed she was saying to me not to grieve too long, but to get on with what God was calling me to do. One scripture I frequently went back to was from the Apostle Paul's letter to Timothy.

> Preach the word; be instant in season, out of season; reprove, rebuke, exhort with all longsuffering and doctrine. For the time will come when they will not endure sound doctrine; but after their own lusts shall they heap to themselves teachers, having itching ears; And they shall turn away *their* ears from the truth, and shall be turned unto fables. But watch thou in all things, endure afflictions, do the work of an evangelist, make full proof of thy ministry.

While I prayed, I asked why this scripture was so important to me now. The more I prayed about it, the more confused I felt. The Spring semester started a week later, and once again I immersed myself in my work. In the back of my mind, that train ride was like an itch I could not seem to scratch.

In June, as students were studying for their finals, I was in the faculty dining room. I sat down at the small table where I had first met Debra. As I ate, I glanced around the room, and I spotted a man who looked vaguely familiar. When he looked at me, I waved, and he walked over. "Hello. Do I know you?"

I shook my head. "Perhaps not. I teach languages in the AddRan School of Liberal Arts. Aren't you one of the professors at Brite Divinity School?"

He nodded. "I'm Elmer Hensen. I got my Ph.D. in New Testament Studies last spring, and I started teaching this past fall. May I join you?"

"Certainly. I was hoping that you would." After he sat down, I resumed. "I have been so busy. I cannot imagine where we have met, but I have a feeling we have."

"Have you been unusually busy?"

"Last summer, I worked on a couple of projects for the war effort, and when I got back from El Paso for a conference, there was a telegram waiting for me telling me that my wife had been killed in London in an automobile accident."

Elmer nodded. "Now, I remember. I went into your house along with two other faculty members. We did not actually speak, but I was there for your wife's impromptu wake."

I nodded. "That explains things. I threw myself into my work to help me deal with – or escape from – my grief. I taught three classes of speaking Japanese, along with four other classes on reading and speaking other languages. I also took three classes to help me work on my B.A. in music."

Elmer's eyes grew wide. "That's an impossible load!"

I nodded again. "You're right, but my grief was shoved into the background. A Navajo Marine friend invited me to join him for skiing in Taos over the Christmas break, and going downhill at breakneck speeds finally put my grief into perspective."

Elmer shook his head. "I've never heard such a story."

I smiled. "Now I know why the Lord wanted our paths to cross today."

"Really? How so?"

"Coming home, I rode in a Pullman Car compartment from Durango to Fort Worth. My deceased wife seemed to be enjoying the ride with me. In my worship times, I kept coming back to the same scripture, but I honestly do not know why."

"What scripture is that?"

"2 Timothy 4:2-5."

Elmer closed his eyes a moment. "We've just met, so I don't know how you will take my response, but here it is. It seems to me as though God is tugging you on your sleeve."

"Tugging on my sleeve???"

"Yes. When God speaks to us, it is seldom through an audible voice, writing in the sky, or some other miracle. God simply gives us a nudge, or a tug on our sleeve. I suggest that, instead of getting your B.A. in music, that you change your major to Religion and take a few classes at Brite. See how your spirit reacts to taking those classes. You're here at the university anyway. Why not?"

That turned out to be the next turning point in my life. That young professor was very wise in his understanding of that passage, as well as Christ-centered enough to guide me effectively. As I began to take classes at Brite Divinity School, my spirit began to be more at peace than it had been when I first met Sileas in Cardigan.

The newspapers were painting a positive picture of the Second World War, but, in my prayers, I knew that those stories did not give us the whole picture. The more I prayed, the more empowered I felt as I taught classes. It seemed as though my classes at Brite, preparing for my future, was the frosting on my life's cake.

In the summer of 1945, the celebration was campus-wide as the war in Europe came to a close. Though no one mentioned the war in the Pacific, deep in my heart, I knew that the rest of the war would be over soon. It was.

Several years later, when I was asked if I had ever heard from my draft board, I said no. There was no record of my birth anywhere except in old Scotland. It might not have survived the Thirty Years' War.

Because I changed my major to religion, it took me another two years to complete my Bachelor's degree. Elmer insisted that University Christian Church should ordain me to Christian ministry, and they did, but I had no sense of what I should do next, except to continue teaching.

With the war being over, my class load had been reduced to that of any full professor. (If I had printed a resume, it probably would have looked impressive!) I continued to teach, and the years flew by.

I began to go to a beauty salon, and each time I got my hair shampooed and cut, I had a few streaks of grey added. From time to time, I was asked to preach, and I gladly said yes. I saw preaching the gospel as a welcome change of pace from my routine at the university.

At the homecoming football game in 1952, I was invited to join the chancellor in his box at the top of Amon G. Carter Stadium. We had become friends, in part because I could speak Gaelic. He had spent his teen years in Ireland, and he enjoyed speaking it. His phone rang in the box, and after speaking very softly for a few moments, he turned to me. "You'll have to excuse me. I'll be back in a few minutes."

I continued to sit, alone in the box, in a very comfortable seat. Two hands appeared on my shoulders, and I felt a warmth flowing through me like a river. I knew it was the angel. "Relax, Brianan. You know who I am. Just enjoy the game while I talk."

I was totally at peace. I was wide awake, yet I was as relaxed as I could be.

"You are ready for God to use you in a special way. Announce your retirement from TCU. Then buy a car and begin driving west. Each Saturday, you will be in a town that needs someone to preach in a church on Sunday morning. The holy spirit will guide you. God will use you as his prophet on Sunday mornings, and on Mondays you will drive west. Eventually, you will be in California, where you will shave your head and then let it grow out again.

In California, at times you will feel led west, other times northward; sometimes you'll go south, and a few times you'll go east. You will be God's prophet as you travel. You will not merely prophesy. Sometimes you will teach, and a few times you will heal."

I was curious. "How long will I do this?"

A surge of warmth flowed through me. "Excellent! You're accepting this on faith. You will make many friends, but you must never backtrack because you will leave behind enemies as you go. You will marry again after a few decades, but she will appear to outlive you. Do not be afraid. You are the Creator's cherished child."

I no longer felt the angel's hands, and a moment later the door opened. The chancellor returned. "I wasn't needed after all." My time with the angel had seemed like ten minutes, but the stadium's clock for play said only a minute had passed.

I let myself be guided by prayer. In the middle of the Spring semester, I told the Chancellor that I was ready to retire, and that it was my final semester. Most people assumed that, with mostly grey hair I was at least seventy, though I did not I state my age. Since I had never gotten a driver's license, I had not gone on record with a birthday.

There were very nice retirement parties. I signed the deed for my house over to the university. It was next to the campus by that time. I bought a big, bulky, gas-guzzling Cadillac, and I sold all but a few keepsakes. I drove west.

+ + +

Whenever I gave a prophecy, it seemed to be a voice from within me that I heard. I cannot explain it in any other way except that way. I often wondered about the meaning of what I said, and then a few days later I would know. Some were rather minor announcements of coming events, but some of the events were major.

The beginning of the Korean War did not begin for nearly week after I proclaimed it. Albert Einstein warned of mutual destruction in the case of nuclear war just two days after I declared it in a small-town pulpit. Headlines said that the states had ratified the 19th amendment the week after I heard myself say it. The first polio vaccine was announced the day after I heard myself tell about it.

In 1954, I heard myself predict the Supreme Court decision known as Brown versus the Board of Education. The elders of that church said they never wanted to see me again, and that week it became law. In 1957, I heard myself saying that Russia would put a satellite into orbit. By the time they did, two days later, I had driven west. Also in 1957, I heard myself warn that a dictator would take over Cuba.

In May of 1961, I entered California, preached on the Exodus, and predicted that we would land a man on the moon by the end of the decade. President Kennedy spoke of landing on the moon at the end of the decade that evening.

In June of 1967, I was on the north side of Bakersfield, California, having breakfast at Rancho Bakersfield, when a man approached my table. "Excuse me, are you not Brianan Tudor?"

I nodded. "I am, sir, and have we met?"

He shook his head. "We have not met until now. I am Charles Tudor, son of James Tudor of Oakland. Most people call me Charlie. May I sit down?"

I grinned, stood up, and shook his hand. "Please do sit down, Charlie. Will you allow me to buy your breakfast?"

"I'd be honored." He sat down. "If you'll permit me, I'll bring you up to date on my part of our family."

I nodded. A waitress approached us, and we placed our orders. I smiled. "I left Oakland a long time ago."

He also nodded. "That is true. My Dad's first wife, Mary, went to work in the San Francisco shipyard after you left, and she was killed in a freak accident there. My Dad went crazy. He drank too much, and he often got into brawls in the bars he went to. The rest of the family went off to the war, and most of them died overseas. My Dad became an impossible man, I'm told, and your grandchildren were raised by in-laws."

I shook my head. "He might have gotten that from me. I've never handled death in the family very well."

He shook his head. "Just before Dad died five years ago, he said that he thought he had gotten his temper from both sides of the family. He was a hundred and one. ... Anyway, like many people, he played the stock market during the twenties and lost it all. In the thirties, he volunteered in soup kitchens. When Dad was eighty-one and working in a soup kitchen in San Diego, an actress named Sarah Cankle came to volunteer. She had made just one movie, but the critics liked her. I must tell you, even her friends always said that she had a screw loose somewhere in her head. She was nineteen when she met Dad, and evidently, she fell in love with him that first day, white hair and all. They got married eight months later, and I was born nine months after that!"

My eyes must have looked like goggles. "Wow! That's quite an age difference." I immediately sensed the irony of saying that to him, but I said nothing further about it.

Charlie grinned and nodded. "My brother, James, was born a year later. We're both in our twenties now. I've a wonderful wife named Janelle, who I married t years ago. We met when I was searching for you. Dad told me the family secret on my eighteenth birthday. My wife and I live in Long Beach. James lives in Monterey, and he's still a bachelor."

Our food came, and after the waitress left, I told him about my journeys in the southwest and my times in Fort Worth until I headed west to preach. I did not share the angel's visits with him. "Give me your address, Charlie, and I'll write to you once in a while."

He wrote it down. "Grand-dad, what do you think is next for you?"

I shook my head. "I never know. The Lord keeps surprising me. Debra's death is finally behind me, so I'll probably marry again. God is continuing to use me"

That first meeting with Charlie was incredibly inspirational. I left that day behind with a new sense of purpose, along with a better sense of my place in God's plans. I wrote him a week later, and when he gave me an address for James, I began to write to him as well. Writing to them every month or two gave me a different kind of perspective on life. I planned to visit them whenever my journey took me to a town nearby.

In July of 1969, just after Neil Armstrong landed on the moon with Ed Aldrin, I opened a post office box in the little town of Coulterville so that I could receive mail as well as send it. As a local address, I used the grocery store. The manager there was a friend. Less than a month later, I received a letter from Charlie, telling me that he and Janelle had two children, with a third on the way. Their oldest was a girl named Samantha, and their second child was a boy, Steven.

On January 21, 1973, I was preaching in a church in Fresno, and I heard myself telling the congregation that the next day, the Supreme Court was going to issue a decision that would trouble the followers of Jesus for many years to come. That Sunday evening I prayed a long time, wondering what that had meant. The next day, the Court ruled on Roe versus Wade. I cried. I traveled south that day, and I ended up the following weekend in the little suburb of Bellflower. After calling Charlie, I had the privilege on Sunday morning of having family members in the congregation while I was preaching. It was a wonderful weekend.

I continued to preach in small towns of California until after the turn of the century. On January 1, 2001, I shaved my head, and after breakfast, I started driving north. Going through Fresno, I veered onto Highway 41 and drove towards Yosemite. I knew there was a chapel there, but when I visited that wondrously beautiful valley, I was not in any way needed at the historic chapel.

In Coulterville, I found letters from Charlie, James, and Charlie's daughter, Samantha. Not stopping to read them, I headed north towards Angels Camp and Sonora. I did not sense any need for my preaching anywhere I went, but in Angels Camp I found lodging for the night. After dinner, I read the letters. It was the first time I had heard from Charlie since before Thanksgiving, and my first letter from James since Memorial Day. The most interesting letter, however, came from

Samantha. It was my first letter from her, and she had many questions.

I put my sons' letters in my suitcase, deciding to answer them later in the week. I estimated that Samantha had already graduated from high school. Remarkably, her communication style was similar to that of her grandmother, Jacqueline. It was well after midnight before I finished my answering letter. It was the beginning of a significant friendship, where we would be corresponding almost monthly.

Leaving Angels Camp the next morning, I went west. My mind floated to many subjects as I drove, and I prayed on behalf of many people who came to mind. I did not stop for lunch, and late in the afternoon, I found myself entering Oakland. I had not been there for so many years! I drove up into the hills. The old property was part of a cemetery, as I had heard. I found Jacqueline's marker clean. The area was well attended.

Going down the hill, I drove randomly (so I thought) until I found myself pulling into the parking lot of First Christian Church. Jacqueline and I had attended there weekly, and it looked good. I pulled into the parking lot, hoping that I could go inside and pray. I rang the doorbell at the parking lot door.

"Yes?" The voice was metallic.

"Hi. My name is Brianan, and a long time ago I worshiped here a few times. I am wondering if I can come inside and pray for a few minutes."

"Certainly." The electric lock of the door buzzed, and I opened it. A woman with grey hair came out of a hallway door and greeted me, and an older African-American woman was with her. "My name is Janice. I'm the church's secretary. This is Margaret, one of the members of the church. Margaret will walk with you down the hall to the sanctuary."

Margaret looked at him. "I've been a member here forever, and I vaguely recognize you. Did you say your name is Brianan?" we started walking.

"Yes, my name is Brianan Tudor."

"A former pastor, Walter Stephanopoulos, is also here to pray. You may remember him." [*The Gaardian Saga* ©2015]

As we walked into the worship area, an older gentleman approached them. He looked vaguely familiar to me, but I could not place him. He stood up, and as I approached, he extended his hand to shake it. "Hello, Brianan, it has been a long time!"

I nodded. "Yes, it has."

Margaret touched Walter's arm. "I have things to do in the office if you need me."

Walter smiled. "Of course, Margaret, thank you." He turned to me. "You may or may not recognize me, Brianan. Let's sit down for a few minutes." We sat down in the front row of seats, near a large acoustic grand piano.

I shook my head slightly. "I have a sense that I've seen you before, but I don't think we have ever spoken."

Walter nodded. "That's correct, Brianan. As I was praying a few moments ago, God revealed your approach to the church to me. We both have special gifts."

I blinked, and I was suddenly aware of who Walter was. "You are Earth's Gaardian. You are fully human and born here in California, but your powers come from some who are not human."

Walter nodded. "Others here are not to know that. Your life is being extended an exceedingly long time, and you can speak any language that fully touches your awareness."

I smiled. "I've not heard it put that way before, but it is true. Furthermore, I can keep a secret."

Walter looked at me directly. "The church building here is fairly large, but the congregations that worship here are small. One of the congregations was larger when I was the pastor here late in the twentieth century. That was more than thirty years ago. Before you leave, stop, and talk to Janice. You're needed on Sunday. She prints a Sunday bulletin. She will want you to spell out your name, and if you have a scripture and sermon title you would like printed, you can give it to her."

I smiled. "All that God does, God does well."

Walter laughed. "I like to say that as well, and I have been saying it for decades! It is time for me to leave. Perhaps we will meet again soon." He vanished.

Startled, I stared at the space where had been. I then closed my eyes and prayed silently. I was totally at peace.

After about a half an hour, I went back down the hall and stopped in the office. "Janice, Walter told me that you need someone to preach this Sunday, and he suggested that I do so. I have no sermon title or scripture for you. I will simply let the Holy Spirit lead me." I spelled my name for her.

Sunday after worship and a soup and sandwich luncheon, I headed east again. The rest of that week I traveled, going as far south as Shaver Lake, and going as far north as Arnold. Several times, I passed through a place called simply called Towne, but I did not stop. [Tom's Town ©2015 and *Soul Mates* ©2016]

I decided to stop and spend the night. After checking into a room, I drove up the highway to a place called Bill's Bar and Grill. Inside it was informal and rustic, but obviously clean and well-maintained. I found a booth and sat down.

A waitress approached. "Good evening, sir, my name is Brooke. Would you like a menu?"

When I looked up at her, I suddenly found myself swimming in her eyes. I nodded. "I'd like a menu, ice water, and a glass of Cabernet."

She smiled. "The house Cabernet is quite good, but if you would like something specific, I can bring you our wine list."

I was still lost in her eyes. I managed to say, "The house Cabernet will be fine."

She smiled again, looking directly at me. "I'll be right back."

Having been happily married four times prior to then, I knew my symptoms. I closed my eyes, and I let myself be present to God's presence. Silently, my spirit clearly sensed one word. "Yes."

This was unlike my experiences with Dearbhail, Sileas, Jacqueline or Debra. Images floated through my mind of our stepping inside one another and walking within one another.

Brooke came back with the wine. "Here's your Cabernet. Taste it, and see if you like it."

I drank a sip. "It's fine."

"What would you like to eat?"

"What do you recommend? I know that's a common question, but if you yourself had to pick between three, what would they be?"

Smiling, she cocked her head and thought. "I'll name four. If I were in the mood for beef, our prime rib is the best in at least three counties, and our Porterhouse steaks are aged and smoked. If I wanted poultry, our chef fixes a game hen that is amazing. Finally, if I were in the mood for fish, we have some fresh steamed halibut with a smoked paprika glaze."

I raised my eyebrows. "For a small town, that's quite a selection!"

"We have a reputation to maintain."

"Okay, I've narrowed it down to the halibut or the game hen."

"Go for the halibut, while we have it. You can get the game hen tomorrow."

Her assuming that I'd be back the next night was not lost on me. It was uncanny.

The halibut was outstanding, and the mincemeat pie with homemade ice cream was a real treat. When I wasn't putting a fork in my mouth, I watched Brooke, but I tried not to stare.

She brought me my check. "Will there be anything else this evening?"

"My name is Brianan Tudor, and I'm a Christian gentleman who has been doing some preaching lately. Would you like to go for a walk with me tomorrow morning?"

She wrote on a piece of paper. "Downtown, the best breakfasts are at The Little Red Hen. I'll see you there at 8:00." She winked and walked off. I was smitten, and I later learned that she was too.

For three months, we had a whirlwind romance. We went to church together on Sundays. We spent all her days off together, taking turns going places that interested one or both of us. I ate at Bill's every day that she worked. On Easter Sunday, I asked her to marry me, giving her an engagement ring with a three-carat diamond surrounded with sapphires. Chao Lee was gone, but his son was a manufacturing jeweler who did excellent work.

Throughout our getting to know one another, I tried to make it clear that I wanted to maintain a separation from my family. She smiled. "Good! My family – what's left of it – is mostly drug addicts and alcoholics. I send them Christmas cards with no return address and mail them from Oakhurst."

I nodded. "That sounds like a good strategy. My family is nice enough, and I have a good relationship with one that calls me Grand-dad because when she was a little girl, her Dad told me that's who I was."

"Grand-dad? You're too young to be a grandfather!"

I smiled. "Nevertheless, if I stay in close contact with anyone from my family – including Samantha, we might be manipulated into situations we would not like. As I said, they're basically good people, but I want to be cautious."

I told her just enough to make it all real. She understood, and it was sufficient for her. She suggested that I continue to correspond with the family using the post office box in Coulterville. Samantha was the one who most often used the box anyway. Brooke had met her, and she liked Samantha as much as I did.

We sent out wedding invitations using an Oakhurst return address supplied by a lawyer friend. We were mysterious about where we would be living after our honeymoon. After getting a wedding license, and after getting a wedding permit from the National Park Service, we invited people to join us for our nuptials at Tenaya Lake in Yosemite. We also had a fire permit, and Bill's catered the reception right there at the lake.

There was never a more scenic wedding, and there was never a more beautiful bride. The first time we went for a walk together, she asked me if I had ever visited any other countries. I told her that I had come from the British Isles when I was much younger. Her face had lit up, and she told me that she had always wanted to visit Scotland, Ireland, and Iceland.

We went to Iceland for our honeymoon. Brooke was easily the most passionate woman I'd ever known. I have no doubt that when we returned to Towne, she was pregnant. She wanted to continue striving toward that goal, even if the doctor told her that she was already with child.

Our first son, Daniel, was born the following March. He was a big baby, taking after me. He had his mother's hair and eyes, and he had my frame and features. Our church family was his family. Brooke and I did not tell our families.

12.
Into the Future

Backtracking a little for my readers, Brooke and I loved Iceland. By the time we landed at Reykjavík, I had decided that Brooke needed to know everything from the beginning. We did not leave our room at the 101 Hotel for the first two days we were there except for meals. Then we began our touring and took many pictures. After dinner on our third evening there, we found a spot where we could just talk quietly.

"Brooke, there are a couple of things about me that you don't know, and it is important that you do know."

"Okay."

"I have two unusual gifts. The first is in terms of languages. A few moments ago, you heard me speak to a bell hop in Icelandic."

Brooke smiled. "I heard that. When did you pick up those phrases?"

I shook my head. "I've not just picked up phrases. I can speak it fluently. Watch." I picked up the phone and pushed the zero. In Icelandic, I spoke for a few minutes, and then I hung up. Brooke was staring at me, wide-eyed. "I asked the front desk about dinner this evening, and they told me. Then I asked about the weather forecast for tomorrow, and they answered. A long time ago I taught languages at TCU. If we were to stay here another week or two, I would be able to teach Icelandic and be competent at it. Give me a month, and I would be able to teach the written language as well."

Brooke's mouth hung open, then she closed it. "Is it the gift of tongues that the Bible talks about?"

I shook my head. "I don't think so. I think glossolalia is a different thing entirely."

"Wow!" She was thoughtful. She looked into my eyes, and for a moment, I dove into hers and went swimming. "You said something about having two gifts. What's the other gift? Is it just as spectacular?"

I nodded, and I described my first encounter with the angel in the warehouse in Scotland. "Believe it or not, my beloved Brooke, that was in 1642."

She stared at me in disbelief. "You have got to be kidding!"

I shook my head. The next time the angel appeared, it was June of 1700, but I'm getting ahead of myself. That first appearance of the angel was after my first wife had died, and our children were grown and had left the nest. My first wife's name was Dearbhail. It was a good marriage, and we had several children, but I was never in love with her. Shall I continue?"

She nodded, so I took her hands and continued to look straight at her. "I followed the angel's instructions and moved to Cardigan. There I fell in love and married a beautiful redhead named Sileas. We were married for well over sixty years, I think. In June of 1700, the angel appeared to the two of us, and Sileas died two years later. I sailed for New York, but I was shipwrecked on the southern coast of this country. The family I stayed with spoke English. When you and I got here three days ago, that was the first time I heard Icelandic in all these years. I sailed to Boston the following Spring, and then I began to explore this country, but avoiding most of the Revolutionary War."

I took a deep breath. "I grieved for Sileas for a very long time. Just before our Civil War began in 1861, I was in South Dakota. I rescued a very young French girl named Jacqueline. She was a mail-order bride who had missed her connection. She heard that her groom had moved to Yellowstone, and since I was going to Yellowstone, we traveled together. We met some Shoshone Indians, and I discovered my gift for languages. When we got to Yellowstone, the man who had sent for her had married someone else."

I cleared my throat. "We were headed west, and she did not want to be alone. Without telling one another, we had fallen in love during our journey. I took out my Geneva Bible, and we said our vows to one another. That marriage lasted until the San Francisco earthquake in 1906, when she was killed."

I blinked a few times. "Once again, I was devastated. I was an established translator in the bay area, so I tried to immerse myself in work, but it was no good. A friend with the railroads asked me to go on staff in Las Vegas as a translator. That was a terrible move. I went west to St. George, Utah, and I did some wandering among Zion Canyon, Bryce Canyon, and the Grand Canyon. I want to take you to the Grand Canyon, Brooke. I'm helplessly and hopelessly in love with you, and there's lots I'd love to share with you."

"Assuming that all you've told me is true, you're over four hundred years old! Four hundred thirty? I love you too, Brianan, but this is a lot to take in!"

"One thing about my history that you may find interesting is this: I'm the illegitimate son James VI of Scotland, who was also James I of Britain. He left that house in Cardigan to me."

"The angel has never said you'd live forever, did she?"

"No. God has simply used me over an extended period of time, using me to bless people. I might live a normal life span with you, and we may grow old together."

Brooke smiled, and her eyes sparkled. "I like that idea, Brianan. I see now why you need to stay disconnected with the other part of your family. What about Samantha? You have not told me about what happened after you spent time at the Grand Canyon. You also haven't told me about your life before the angel first appeared."

For the rest of our honeymoon, I filled in the gaps of my life for her, and I answered all the questions she asked. For the first time during my long life, I shared all of me with someone, even more than my history. I shared my heart as I had not done previously, ever. Sometimes it was difficult, and Brooke expressed open wonder at some of the decisions I had made. When we got home to Towne, we were truly one in God's spirit.

Brooke suggested that, since I did not keep a diary, that perhaps I should write out my entire story and keep it in an encrypted file. I could then pass it on to our oldest child. Inasmuch as I wanted to have many children with her, and since our first had not yet been born, the suggestion was a blessing in itself.

I continue to write to Samantha, but I know that my time for closure is almost here. My marriage to Brooke marks a significant turning point in my life. I am truly blessed. Our first son, Daniel, is growing like a weed. Brooke is pregnant again, and we think it might be twins.

Brooke still enjoys working part time, when she's not pregnant, but she's no longer working at Bill's Bar and Grill. One of her bosses there wrote a letter of recommendation, and she's working at another restaurant in another community.

God is at work, and I'm still being used for the glory of the Lord. I don't know if I will grow old (finally) with Brooke, but I'm ready for whatever God has prepared for me.

Epilogue

You've finished reading Grand-dad's story. Everyone except me is certain that he died in that huge explosion set off by terrorists in San Diego, even though his body wasn't found. When I got back from his memorial service at Towne Community Church, I found a file hidden in my bedroom closet on a disk, along with a personal and private letter to me. Grand-dad kept his promise. This book is based upon that file. If anyone but my beloved Grand-dad Brianan had written both this book and that letter, I wouldn't have believed it.

As he said at the beginning, I'm not stupid, and I know that virtually every chapter of this book is totally impossible. The trouble is, I knew Grand-dad better than anyone else in the family, and I have an uncanny feeling that every word of it is true. I don't expect you or anyone else to believe that, and I am probably the only one that does.

I remember the day that Grand-dad said he was going to go home in a year or two. If he was actually killed in that explosion, Grand-dad has gone home to heaven. That means he's with his first four wives, and he left Brooke behind. I have absolutely no idea where Brooke is or how to reach her, except perhaps through the post office box. She no longer works at Bill's Bar and Grill in Towne, and they say they don't know where she has moved. So far, I've not heard from her.

If Grand-dad was not killed, he might have gone home to Belfast, where his Mum got pregnant with him, or to Linlithgow in Scotland where he grew up, unless he's still in California with Brooke. Next summer, my husband and I are going to spend a month in the British Isles. Maybe we'll see him.

After reading the file this book is based on, my uncle James told me he wanted to publish it as a novel. I'm letting him do that. He's the listed author. If you need to be critical or complain, it's on his head. I'm out of this now. When I get to heaven, I'm going to have a lot of questions for my Grand-dad.

Other Books by James J. Stewart
Available at Amazon.com

Christian Fiction

The Gaardian Saga
[Christian Science Fiction Fantasy with multiple romances]

Casting Lots
[Young Adults Cast Lots to Hear from God in the Near Future]

Tom's Town
[Small Town Life and Romance in California's Sierra Foothills]

Soul Mates
[Another Romance in the same setting as *Tom's Town*]

Prayer Warriors
[Prayers and Miracles in a Near-Future Continuation of *Casting Lots*]

Christian Poetry and Inspiration

Faith and Yosemite
[Christian poetry with pictures of Yosemite]

Faith Fuel
[Meditations]

Lasting Love
[Short Biographical Sketches]

Walking in Faith
[The same poetry as *Faith and Yosemite*, with more, but without pictures]

Seed Thoughts for Christian Prayer and Meditation
[Workbook]

Living for Jesus
[Bible Study Guide for Couples and Small Groups]

Deliberately Growing Spiritually
[A Bible-reading sequence for intentional spiritual growth]

Yosemite Picture Books

Ever-Changing Yosemite Valley

Faith and Yosemite
[see the above poetry]

Portraits of El Capitan

Portraits of Half Dome

Starlight Over Yosemite

Yosemite Textures and Shadows